S0-CGP-849

DATE DUE

Bill Reno

THE BADGE SERIES

THE BLACK COFFIN

G.K. HALL & CO.
Boston, Massachusetts
1989

Library of Congress Cataloging in Publication Data

Reno, Bill.
    The black coffin / Bill Reno.
        p.   cm.—(G.K. Hall large print book series)   (Nightingale
    series)
      ISBN 0-8161-4778-7
      1. Large type books.   I. Title.
    [PS3568.E637B5   1989]
    813'.54—dc19   88-32277

THE BLACK COFFIN

The lone rider slipped from his saddle in the high country of Colorado amid the long shadows of the towering pines. Adjusting the twin Colt .45s on his narrow hips, the tall blond gunslinger gazed for a moment at the setting sun. The jagged, saw-toothed peaks seemed to bite into the orange ball of fire.

He made camp in the Rocky Mountain timber some five miles south of the town known as Central City. The muscular blue-eyed man relieved his buckskin gelding of the saddle and led him to a nearby stream. While the animal took its fill, the tall rider gathered sticks for a fire.

It was totally dark when Dave Bradford washed his tin plate and cup in the stream and cleaned up the skillet. The wind whined in the tops of the tall trees as he lay down under a blanket on a soft bed of pine needles, resting his head on the saddle. The scent of the surrounding pine was pleasant to his nostrils.

Somewhere out in the vast darkness a lone wolf howled mournfully for its mate. No answer came. The pitiful cry was repeated, but still there was no answer. Then all was quiet.

Dave thought how he had much in common with that poor beast out there in the darkness. He, too, was a lone wolf. The haunting cry of the wolf echoed through the mountains again. "Too bad, old boy," Dave said aloud. "Sounds like your girl must've left you."

A tinge of loneliness sent a chill through his body. A few times in his travels Dave had met some decent young woman. Any one of them would have made him a good wife. He had felt himself falling in love a couple of times, but quickly rode away, depriving himself of that luxury. What kind of a life could a drifter like him offer a young woman?

With the pain of loneliness clawing at his heart, the blond man drifted off to sleep.

Daylight was murky over the jagged Rockies when Dave Bradford heard the big buckskin gelding nicker. Suddenly sensing danger, he opened his pale blue eyes. Having removed his gun belt, Dave had laid both .45s next to his hips under his blanket, and now his hands instinctively closed around the cool grips.

A sharp voice cut the early morning air, confirming his hunch. "Hold it right there!"

Dave blinked and focused on his intruders. There were three of them standing in a broken semicircle. He saw only two horses. The man who had spoken held a revolver on him. Another had his gun in hand. The third had not bothered to draw his gun.

"Now let's see them hands come out from under that blanket nice and easy," said the gunman. "All we want is your horse. You'll live if you do what we tell you."

Dave had been in tight spots before. Quickly he analyzed the situation. The two men with guns drawn would have to be disposed of first. The other one stood near them.

His gunfighter's nerves livened with electricity. The man was about to speak again when Dave moved like a deadly diamondback. Double lances of flame shot through the blanket. Booming reverberations shook the air as the gun slipped from the suddenly loosened grip of the spokesman. The man crumpled earthward, shock whitening his features.

Releasing his left-hand Colt, Dave quickly rolled out of the blanket. Like the wings of a hummingbird his free hand fanned the hammer of the big gun in his right hand. The .45 boomed and belched fire, spitting instant death for the one swinging the muzzle on him and wounding the other one, who was clawing for his gun. The one still alive rolled over in the pine needles.

Dave was aware of the rumbling sound of more horses as he stood and walked toward the fallen gunman, a thin thread of smoke lifting from his muzzle. The wounded man was young, Dave noticed. Maybe twenty.

As Dave drew near, the young outlaw raised to one knee and started to lift his revolver. "Drop it, kid!" Dave snapped, lining his Colt on him. He cocked it with a warning flourish.

Teeth bared in agony, the kid froze momentarily, eyeing the tall man with venom. Then, bracing the revolver in both hands, he tried to steady himself as he thumbed back the hammer. He shakily raised the pistol at Dave and hissed, "You die—"

Dave's .45 roared. The slug entered the kid's face right between the eyes. His revolver hit the ground and discharged harmlessly. Only seconds later Dave was surrounded by riders leaping from their saddles.

"Good work, big fellow!" exclaimed a silver-haired, mustached man, who was no runt himself. "My name's Morey Barrigan. I own the Barrigan Mining Company over at Georgetown."

"Hate to kill a kid," Dave said morosely, staring at the corpse.

"This here's a posse, son," continued Barrigan. "These outlaws held up our bank yesterday. Killed our town marshal—three other citizens too." Barrigan looked around as the posse members examined the bodies. He swore and said, "You men see what this fellow did? Wiped out the whole gang single-handed!"

A handsome red-haired man in his twenties gathered up Dave's gun belt and the other Colt. Extending them to the tall man, he said, "Here you go, mister. That was some kind of shooting! My name's Derek Sheffield."

"Howdy," said Dave with a tight smile, accepting the gun and belt.

As Dave buckled on the guns and thonged them to his thighs, Sheffield turned around and directed the nine other men of the posse in picking up the bodies. One of the men stared at Dave for a long moment, then began ransacking the outlaws' saddlebags.

"Derek is my son-in-law, mister," Barrigan said to Dave. "He's my business manager at the mine."

Dave nodded.

"I didn't catch your name," said the mineowner.

Just as Dave was about to speak the man digging in the saddlebags hollered, "Here's the money, Morey!" Hurrying toward the white-haired Barrigan with a canvas bag in his hands, he said, "Looks like it's all here. Guess they didn't stash any along the way."

"Good!" Barrigan smiled. "Mr. Anderson will be happy about that." Turning to Dave, he said, "Carl Anderson is the president of the bank."

"Oh." Dave nodded.

"This is Alf Boggs," said Barrigan, pointing to the man who held the money bag. "I still don't knows yours."

Before Dave could speak, Alf Boggs smiled wide and blurted, "I know his name, Morey. This here's the famous Dan Starr! Fastest man on God's green earth with a pair o' irons! I seen him use 'em before in

6

San Antonio." Pointing to the three corpses being loaded on two horses, he added, "Ain't nobody but Dan Starr coulda done that!"

"Dan Starr, eh?" said the mineowner, looking Dave in the eye.

This wasn't the first time that Dave had been mistaken for his twin brother, Dan Starr—a man who was lightning with a gun but had always walked on the right side of the law.

Dave thought it best to allow Boggs's mistake to stand. If word got around that Dave Bradford was involved in a shoot-out in these parts, it might reach the ears of the U.S. marshal in Denver. The law would be hot on his trail again.

Dave chuckled. "Guess a fellow can't even go for the high country without being recognized."

"Heard a lot about you, Starr," said Barrigan, gripping Dave's hand. "They say you're faster than a weaver's shuttle." Eyeing the bodies draped over the horses, he added, "Now I believe it!"

Derek Sheffield stepped in, eyes wide. "Is Alf pulling my leg, mister, or are you really Dan Starr?"

"Was the last time I looked in the mirror," said Dave with a casual tone.

Turning to the others, Sheffield hollered, "Alf isn't kidding, boys! He says he *is* Dan Starr!"

Quickly the others gathered around, eyes roving over the tall, handsome man with twin Colts thonged to his thighs. One by one they shook Dave's hand and introduced themselves. When they had finished, Morey Barrigan stroked his silver mustache and said, "I suppose they jumped you for your horse."

"Yep." Dave nodded. "Least that's what they told me they wanted."

"If they'd only known who they were pickin' on," said one of the posse, shaking his head in disbelief. "They'd have been glad to keep ridin' double!"

Barrigan laughed. Looking at Dave, he said, "We found one of their horses a few miles back. Busted leg. They didn't even have the decency to shoot the poor beast."

"We're ready to ride, Dad," the red-haired Sheffield said to the mineowner.

"Mount up," responded Barrigan. Turning to Dave, he said, "Where you headed, son?"

"Well . . . uh . . . Grand Junction," replied Dave, trying to sound definite.

"Urgent?"

8

"Well . . ."

"There might be a bounty on some of them hombres you just sent to meet their Maker," said the mineowner. "If you ain't in any rush to cross the Divide, why don't you ride into Georgetown with us. We'll take a look through the marshal's posters. Maybe you can pick yourself up some money."

Dave thought of his nearly empty pockets. If there *was* a bounty, it would take several weeks to collect it. But he was only wandering aimlessly anyhow. It was worth a try.

"Sure," said the tall man. "I'll ride along."

"Good!" said Barrigan, cuffing Dave's muscular shoulder. "Let's go!"

As he rode alongside the posse Dave Bradford thought back on the long trail that had put him on one side of the law and his brother on the other.

Born David Bradford Starr on April 23, 1843, he was the identical twin brother of Daniel Blane Starr, and the son of Benjamin and Amy Starr. The boys were raised on a farm near San Angelo, Texas. When they were fifteen years old, their parents, while off on a trip to a nearby town, were killed by renegade Comanche Indians. There was no one left to take care of the boys, so the twins made an attempt at running the farm by themselves.

Within a few months, Dave, deeply troubled by his parents' death, began to have other interests than the hard work involved on the farm. He would ride off and be gone two or three days at a time, leaving the whole load on Dan. His absences caused problems between the brothers. It grew worse when Dan learned that Dave was running with a bad crowd and had been robbing travelers and stagecoaches.

After a bloody fistfight between them, Dave had promised Dan he would straighten up. It lasted a few weeks, then Dave went off on another three-day spree.

Dan, while visiting San Angelo, learned that several banks had been robbed in surrounding towns. He was riding back from San Angelo to the farm when a marshal and posse from one of the towns surrounded him at gunpoint and arrested him as one of the bank robbers. His explanation that the robber was his identical twin brother held no sway with the marshal, and he was jailed. Not until the whole gang was caught in a hideout did the marshal believe Dan's story.

Dave was sentenced to three years in prison at Huntsville. Facing Dan in tears, he said he was sorry and asked Dan to forgive him. Dave went to prison. Dan went back to the farm.

While doing time in the Huntsville prison Dave met an infamous gunslinger named Ed Harmon and they struck up a friendship. When the gunslinger's cronies broke him out of jail, Dave Starr went along.

Dave had never really meant to go bad; it had just happened. To keep his brother from carrying the shame of having an outlaw brother, he had changed his name by dropping the Starr and going by his middle name, becoming Dave Bradford.

Ed Harmon bought Dave Bradford a pair of twin Navy Colts and proceeded to teach the youth the fast-draw. "Learn to use *two* guns, Davey Boy," Harmon would say. "It's almost like being *two* men."

Young Bradford quickly learned that he had a natural knack for the weapons. Running with Harmon, he had ample opportunity to practice against one of the best. He worked on his draw every chance he got, although he did not know if he had the nerve to actually shoot a man face to face.

Dave had become as fast as his teacher

when a seasoned professional named Mel King challenged Ed Harmon outside a saloon in Del Rio, Texas. King dropped Harmon in the dust. In anger, young Dave set his pale blue eyes on the gunslinger and issued his own challenge.

Thinking the tall, lanky kid just another headstrong greenhorn, King went for his gun. In less than a heartbeat Mel King lay in the dust with Ed Harmon . . . and Dave Bradford was now a gunfighter.

At twenty-two Dave weighed two hundred ten pounds and stood six-three before he put on his boots. Broad in the shoulders and narrow in the hips, he let no one push him around and was as good with his fists as with a gun.

Being lonely for his twin, Dave rode home to see him and was surprised to learn that the farm had been sold. Dan had married Sarah Duncan, a San Angelo girl. During the first year of their marriage two gun-slinging drifters had happened by the farm when Dan was in town. They had raped and murdered Sarah.

Dan had strapped on two guns, learned to fast-draw, and gone after them. He had caught them and killed them in a shoot-out. Now Dan Starr, too, was a gunfighter, and he was becoming more famous every day. Greenhorn hopefuls were coming to Texas to challenge him—and were dying under his guns.

The twins crossed paths a few times, but Dan was uncomfortable in the presence of his outlaw brother.

Time moved along. At twenty-six Dave Bradford had graduated to a pair of Frontier Colts and had a price on his head all over Texas. Now, in June 1873 at the age of thirty, Dave was tired of running. Traveling in Colorado and Wyoming, he was at the end of his funds but reluctant to put on a robber's mask once again.

He had thought of giving up the outlaw trail and settling down. Several times he had even tried it, taking jobs as a cowpuncher on some out-of-the-way ranch. But sooner or later someone had shown up to recognize him as Dave Bradford the outlaw. Pulling up stakes, he would move on.

As the posse neared Georgetown Dave thought how nice it would be to sleep in a hotel bed. But he had no cash. Suddenly the thought of that bounty money took on added interest. The day before, he had been considering robbing the bank in either Central City or Georgetown, though the idea actually had been distasteful to the wandering outlaw. His last robbery had been several weeks ago in Rawlins, Wyoming, but had netted him only a little over a hundred dollars. Not long before that in Denver, he had unexpectedly run into Dan. They had talked for a few minutes, then parted. Subsequently Dave had ridden north, robbed the Rawlins bank, then hightailed it back south into the Colorado Rockies. He hated to stir up the law against himself in these parts. *Like it or not*, Dave told himself, *you'll have to do something soon if there's no bounty.*

Georgetown, booming because of Morey Barrigan's gold strike, was a beehive of activity when the posse and Dave Bradford rode in just before noon. Miners were being hired by the Barrigan Company as fast as they hit the place. Some came with families, while others bunked three or four men in each of the makeshift shacks that were being erected along the banks of the river that flowed through the town.

Dave noted that the town's two established saloons, the Red Rose and the Big Buffalo, were now facing competition from several nameless liquor outlets doing business in tents. Their signs promised cut-rate prices.

People thronged around, eyes goggling at the three corpses draped over the horses' backs. The procession hauled up in front of the Georgetown Bank. Questions were being fired from all sides. Morey Barrigan raised his hands, palms forward, while still in the saddle. "Just a minute, folks!" he shouted. "Somebody bring Carl Anderson out here. I want him to hear this while I tell all of you!"

In less than a minute the tall, slender bank president, a man in his sixties, appeared in the doorway. A broad smile transformed his face as he spotted the canvas bag held by Alf Boggs, then the three bank robbers bellied down in death.

"Good work, Morey!" exclaimed Anderson, shaking his fist. "Maybe this'll make the next bunch that thinks about robbing us think again!"

"Wasn't us that did it, Carl," said Barrigan. Pointing to Dave, astride the big buckskin, he yelled, "This man right here took out the whole gang all by himself, folks!"

Dave blushed as the crowd cheered.

"You know who this man is?" asked the mineowner. "Take a good look!"

Dave wished that he had ridden the other way as the curious onlookers pressed close, squinting at the tall man's tanned face.

"It's Dan Starr!" came a young female voice.

A sudden hush came over the throng as the woman pushed herself through the press. The name Dan Starr was whispered among the gathered citizens of Georgetown. Dave's nervous gaze focused on the strikingly beautiful face of a blonde clad in a gingham dress. On her perfectly formed figure the gingham seemed to turn to exquisite silk.

She approached close enough to touch him, looked up with alluring blue eyes, and said, "Hello, Dan. It's been a long time."

II

Dave Bradford felt his spine chill. This woman was a friend of Dan Starr's. His ruse was over. He had already thought about the possibility of one of his own posters being among the others in the marshal's

16

office. He was trying to work his tongue loose when the lovely blonde said, "I guess it's been longer than I thought."

"Well . . . I . . ." Dave stammered.

"Jo-Beth Taylor," she said, eyes pleading for recognition. "Don't you remember?"

Dave was about to come clean when Jo-Beth unwittingly released the pressure by saying, "Of course, you were twenty-one and I was only thirteen. Amarillo?"

"Oh, sure!" Dave lied with a chuckle. "I have a dusty recollection!"

"You'll be here for a while?" the blonde asked.

"Guess so," said Dave, still short on words.

"We'll get together and I'll dust off your memory."

"Sure, Jo-Beth." Dave nodded. He was certain she could see right through him. His mind was in a whirl. Could he continue the ruse?

Suddenly there was a clamor for "Dan Starr" to tell the excited crowd how he had shot it out with the bank robbers. Modestly, Dave gave a brief description of the incident.

"Hey!" shouted Morey Barrigan. "I'm buyin' drinks at the Big Buffalo for all the posse, Dan Starr, and Carl Anderson! We got our money back. Let's celebrate!"

The people cheered, then began to return to their workday tasks. Dave watched Jo-Beth Taylor walk away until she disappeared in the crowd, then he dismounted and walked with the mineowner to the Big Buffalo Saloon.

An hour later Dave was led by Morey Barrigan to the office of Marshal Bo Plummer, who had been killed by the outlaws. Derek Sheffield tagged along. As they entered the office Barrigan said, "I think Bo kept the stack of posters here in this file." Stepping to the wooden cabinet, he pulled open a drawer. Rummaging for a moment, he lifted out a six-inch-thick stack of wanted posters. "Here they are, Dan," he said. "Let's each take a bunch and wade through 'em."

Panic clutched at Dave's heart. It was entirely possible that his own picture was in there. Quickly he said, "Did you fellows get a good enough look at those outlaws so you could recognize them?"

Barrigan and Sheffield eyed each other blankly. "Maybe not, Dan," the older man admitted reluctantly.

"Look," said Dave, "you two have probably got plenty to do. Why don't you just leave me here, and I'll leaf through them?"

"Okay," agreed Morey. "Let's go, Derek. We'll come back later."

"Give me a couple hours," said Dave.

"Fine," said Barrigan. "In the meantime we'll have a bed made up for you at my house."

"No, please don't trouble yourself, Mr. Barrigan," Dave protested. "I couldn't do that." His eyes swerved to a cot across the room. "That where the marshal slept?"

"Yes, but—"

"I'll just bed down there, sir."

"But—"

"Really, Mr. Barrigan, I don't want to intrude on you and your family."

"Tell you what then," said the mineowner. "You could stay at Derek's house. My daughter and grandchildren are back east for a visit. Won't be back for better'n two weeks. You and Derek can keep each other company."

"Sure," spoke up Sheffield, "why not? How about it, Dan?"

"Gentlemen," said Dave. "I really appreciate your offer. But I'm a born loner. I'd really be more relaxed staying right here.

At least until the town hires a new marshal. That is, unless you think some of the townspeople would object."

"Hardly," said Barrigan. "You're a hero here. Besides, I'm chairman of the town council. What I say goes, and you're welcome to sleep here if it suits your fancy."

"Thank you, sir," Dave smiled.

"You *will* eat supper with us, won't you?" asked Barrigan. "My wife is some cook."

"Sure. Be honored."

"Fine," said the silver-haired man. "Let's go, Derek."

Dave watched the two men angle across the street, then he carried the stack of posters to the desk and sat down. He tossed his hat onto a chair in the nearest corner and began his task.

About a third of the way through the stack he found a poster with an artist's conception of his own face. There it was:

WANTED

By authorities in El Paso, Fort Worth, and Abilene, Texas. Bank robbery and stagecoach robbery.

DAVE BRADFORD

$1000 Reward

Height . . . 6'3"

Weight . . . 210 lbs.

Hair . . . . . Blond

Eyes . . . . . Blue

Casting a glance toward the door, Dave picked up a match from the desk and lit the corner of the poster. Turning it slowly, he let it burn to a small piece, then dropped it in an ashtray. When there was nothing but ashes, he dumped them into a half-full wastebasket.

As soon as he started flipping posters again he thought of his twin brother. Dan Starr was a legend in his own lifetime. Mr. Lightning. Although Dave was no slouch with a gun, either, how long would he be able to make these people believe he was Dan? Especially that beautiful Jo-Beth Taylor.

Dave frowned and continued flipping posters.

Suddenly there was a familiar face. It was the outlaw who had stood next to that kid this morning. The poster identified him as Brant Curwood. The name rang a bell in the back of Dave's brain. *Curwood . . . Curwood . . .* It came to him as his eyes took in the rest of the poster. Brant Curwood was part of the infamous Curwood family of Lawrence, Kansas. There were eleven children. Nine were boys. Their father and mother were killed before the eyes of the younger ones by Quantrill's raiders one hot August day in 1863.

Within three years the older boys had tracked down eighteen of Quantrill's men and slaughtered them. The thrill of violence and the taste of bloodshed was ingrained by that time. All nine Curwood boys became outlaws, riding, raiding, and robbing . . . spilling blood, without mercy.

Brant Curwood, thought Dave. *Sure didn't know I was killing a Curwood. He was about forty. Must've been one of the oldest brothers. Some of the others are dead now. . . .*

Dave noted that there was a two-thousand-dollar reward for Brant Curwood, dead or alive. Laying the poster to one side, he looked down at the next one. There was the face of the kid Dave had shot between the eyes. His face stiffened when he read the name. *Jake Curwood!* The posters noted that Brant and Jake, though still in good standing with the eldest brother, the notorious Adam Curwood, were now operating on their own.

Dave picked up the other poster and compared the two faces. They were nothing alike. A person would never take them for brothers. Jake had two thousand dollars on his head also. Fine print at the bottom told Dave to contact the U.S. marshal's office in Topeka. *Four thousand dollars!* That would certainly beef up his sagging financial status.

Setting the Curwood brothers' posters aside, the tall man continued through the stack.

The sun was casting slanted rays in rectangular shapes on the office floor as Dave turned the last poster. There was nothing on the other outlaw. He fitted the stack together and tapped it several times on the desk. Just as he replaced them in the drawer of the file the sound of angry voices came from somewhere out on the street.

Curious, Dave donned his dark brown flat-crowned Stetson and stepped out onto the board sidewalk. A crowd was gathering around two men who were shouting at each other heatedly in front of the general store. Ambling up the street, Dave saw that one of the men was a big bruiser—looked to be about six feet, but probably weighed at least two-eighty. The other one was about the same height, but of slender build. Both appeared to be in their middle twenties.

Two men dashed past Dave. "Chris John and Frederick Lobdell," said one to the other. "Looks like Chris has finally got his fill."

"Yeah, but Lobdell will kill him," commented the other one.

Dave looked over the heads of the encircling crowd as the two young men warily faced each other in the middle of the street.

"Oh, dear Lord," said one middle-aged woman to another, "I wish Marshal Plummer was here! Lobdell will beat him to death!"

Dave wondered if the town had anyone to keep the peace in the dead marshal's place. He spotted Morey Barrigan and his son-in-law on the other side of the crowd. At the same moment he saw Jo-Beth Taylor appear in the door of the Alpine Café.

Christopher John's face was beet red. "I've told you to stay away from Merilee,

Lobdell!" he hissed through bared teeth. "She's my wife, and I don't care how big you are—I'm not putting up with it!"

"Smack him, Fred!" hollered a hefty man not much smaller than Lobdell, and about the same age.

Chris's eyes flicked to the man, past Lobdell's burly shoulder. "You stay out of it, Leonard!" he snapped.

Leonard Whaley sprayed saliva as he rasped in return, "Sweep up the street with him, Fred!"

It didn't take Dave long to spot Merilee John. She stood on the inner fringe of the crowd, her eyes wide, face blanched. Trembling fingers nervously touched her cheeks. Small of frame, she looked like a frightened little girl. With tremulous voice she said, "Let's go home, Chris. Please!"

Chris's eyes stayed riveted to those of Frederick Lobdell. Without turning, he said, "Not till this stinking drifter has it through his thick skull that you're my wife, Merilee! And he knows to leave you alone!"

Lobdell's eyes held those of Christopher John. He said huskily, "Don't kid yourself, little man. She likes me flirtin' with her!"

"That's a lie!" screamed Merilee. "I detest you!"

His eyes still fixed on Chris, the big brute laughed and said, "Who do you think you're kiddin', honey? I know what you are!"

Christopher John's fist lashed out as raw fury seared through his body. He caught the big man flush on the mouth, splitting his lip. Lobdell's head snapped back, but he rebounded with a meaty fist that dropped the smaller man to the wagon-rutted street.

Merilee let out a shriek as the monster pounced on her husband. Fists, arms, elbows, knees, and feet flailed as the two men rolled in the dirt. Abruptly John sprang free, blinking against the dust in his eyes. As Lobdell rose, the smaller man popped him on the mouth a second time. Lobdell swung and missed. His bloody mouth caught a flashing fist again.

Dave was feeling good about the way the smaller man was handling himself with the huge brute. The crowd was definitely on Chris's side, cheering him openly.

They traded blows again, and Chris was down. Dave flinched as Lobdell drove a savage boot into Chris's rib cage. The dirty tactic brought jeers from some onlookers.

"Kick his guts out, Fred!" bellowed Leonard Whaley.

The smaller man dodged the next kick

and scrambled to his feet. Twisting to favor the damaged ribs, he lunged at Lobdell and connected on the already ravaged mouth. Both upper and lower lips were split and bloody. Lobdell charged like a bull, bowling his opponent over with his massive body. Breath whooshed from Chris's mouth as the big man landed on top of him.

They rolled, huffed, grunted, and snorted, while Merilee wept and the crowd yelled.

Both men got to their feet, and fists were whistling again. Chris ducked a murderous haymaker and connected with Lobdell's mouth once more.

As Chris John circled the groggy-looking hulk, Leonard Whaley dashed in, seized him, and pinned his arms down. "Hit him now, Fred!" he yelled.

Eyes widened, Lobdell stepped in. He swung a wild punch, connecting with Chris's jaw. Chris went limp, sagging in Whaley's arms.

Nearby, Dave Bradford glowered angrily, his blood hot with rage. Plowing through the crowd, he stepped into the circle and slammed Lobdell with a hissing sledgehammer blow. The husky fighter sailed into the gathered onlookers, who could not backtrack swiftly enough to dodge him. Six or seven men were knocked off their feet.

A malicious grin curled Whaley's thick lips. "So you gonna butt in, eh, blondie?"

"Don't like dirty stuff," snarled Dave.

Whaley dropped the unconscious Chris John and came at the blond man like a freight train. Dave sidestepped and chopped the man savagely behind the ear. People were frantically dragging Chris out of the way as Whaley flopped facedown in the dirt. He staggered to his knees, wagging his ponderous head.

A flicking glance told Dave that Lobdell was still sprawled in the dust, out cold. The fallen onlookers were up and retreating.

Whaley's look was murderous as he found his feet and glared at Dave Bradford. The latter removed his Stetson and sailed it to waiting hands in the crowd. Jo-Beth Taylor moved in and claimed the hat.

"I'm gonna turn you into chopped meat, blondie," Whaley growled.

"You do it, then talk about it," retorted the man who posed as Dan Starr.

"Knock his block off, Dan!" came the voice of one of the men who had been in the posse. "If you can fight like you can shoot, you can do it with one hand!"

28

Whaley came like an angry boar. Dave ducked his swinging fists and drove a steel-piston punch to his belly. A thick grunt of wind billowed from Whaley's lungs as he jackknifed forward. From somewhere near the rutted ground Dave brought an uppercut to the huge man's nose. The blow straightened him up, and Dave fired a stiff left jab to the chin. Whaley sat down hard, shaking his head. Blood ran from his nostrils.

Taking a momentary respite, Dave slipped the Colt .45s from their well-oiled holsters and handed them to Morey Barrigan.

"Teach him a lesson, Dan," said Barrigan, closing his fingers on the grips of the twin Colts.

A mixture of awe and admiration beamed in twenty-two-year-old Jo-Beth's eyes as she took a place beside Barrigan.

Leonard Whaley got up on wobbly legs, lifted a hand, and wiped his bleeding nose. He looked at the hand, then at Dave. A poisonous look filled his eyes. Like a huge, wild beast, Whaley charged. Dave braced himself and shot a fist to the oncoming jaw. Whaley grunted and blinked, swung hard, and missed. Dave hurled another one to the same spot, then another.

Whaley was driven back against the hitching rail, his eyes glazing over. While the people shouted wildly Dave Bradford stepped in and slammed one more blow to the big man's jaw. Whaley's knees buckled. He hung against the rail for a brief moment, then slid to the ground, unconscious.

The ecstatic crowd erupted in a bedlam of cheers, rushing around the tall man. Dave fought his way to a nearby trough and buried his head in the water. Congratulations were heaped upon him as he walked back to where Lobdell was now sitting in the street, dabbing a soiled handkerchief to his battered mouth.

Morey Barrigan stepped in beside Dave as he stood over Lobdell. "You know the way out of town, big fellow?" asked Dave, slipping his guns back in their holsters.

Looking at the bloody handkerchief, Lobdell said, "Yeah."

"Good," said Dave. "Then you go bring your friend to his senses and get out of here before you both have to be carried out."

Lobdell gave the tall man a sullen look, but nodded. "Okay, okay."

Accepting it as a settled matter, Dave strode to the boardwalk, where Merilee John was tending to her bruised husband.

He smiled at the pretty young woman, then said to Chris John, "You all right?"

"Got some mighty sore ribs, Mr. Starr," replied Chris, "but other than that, I think I'm okay."

"That was some handy fighting you did against that gorilla, Chris," said Dave. "You must've spotted him at least a hundred pounds."

Chris smiled in spite of a swollen lip. "From what Merilee tells me, the fighting that went on after my lights went out wasn't too shabby either. I'm beholden to you."

"My pleasure," Dave said with a smile. "That two-against-one stuff irritates my gizzard."

"Thank you, Mr. Starr," said Merilee. "They might have beat Chris to death if you hadn't stepped in." Swinging her gaze to the silver-haired man who stood nearby, she said, "I think we ought to keep him in Georgetown, don't you, Mr. Barrigan?"

"Be the best thing that ever happened to this place," agreed Barrigan.

A small, feminine figure glided up behind Dave and tapped his shoulder. Turning around, he set his pale blue gaze on the captivating face of Jo-Beth Taylor. Extending the flat-crowned Stetson, she said, "Here's your hat, champ."

Dave crimsoned. "Thank you," he said with a grin.

"After a workout like that you're probably hungry," she said. "I work over here at the Alpine Café. Could I buy your supper?"

"Not tonight, Jo-Beth," spoke up Barrigan. "Dan's eating at my house."

Drinking in the young woman's beauty, Dave said softly, "How about breakfast tomorrow morning?"

"Fine." She smiled back. "Breakfast it is. See you then." With that, she turned and floated away.

In the eye of Dave Bradford she seemed to move like a fairy princess.

Morey Barrigan's wife was some cook, Dave thought as he sat down at the lavishly spread table. "Sure looks good, ma'am," he remarked. "I think I'm hungry enough to eat it all."

"You just dig in, Dan," said Dottie Barrigan warmly.

Dave sat at the opposite end of the table from the handsome silver-haired owner of the Barrigan Mining Company. On Barrigan's right sat Emily, their twenty-year-old daughter. Emily was lovely and a fully developed young woman. Next to Emily was sixteen-year-old Brett, who very much resembled his father.

Across the table from Brett sat Derek Sheffield, who was taking his evening meals with his in-laws while Shirley Barrigan Sheffield was in Kansas City with Derek's parents. The paternal grandparents had not seen little Timmy since he was a year old, which was four years ago. Shirley had taken him and their seven-month-old Theresa to visit the Sheffields for a month. Dottie Barrigan sat next to the red-haired Sheffield.

Dave looked down to see a big, shaggy black-and-white dog slip into the dining room and drop to his haunches beside Brett Barrigan. Dottie eyed Brett warily. "Don't you do it, boy," she warned.

"Who, me?" asked Brett in an innocent tone.

Dave eyed mother and son quizzically.

Dottie smiled. "Mutt knows Brett will slip him some goodies if he hangs around," she explained. "I've been trying to train both boy and dog for six years. Mutt should eat at his own mealtime, not ours."

"But, Mom," argued Brett, "he feels left out if he doesn't dine with the family."

Dottie rolled her eyes heavenward. "See what I mean?"

Dave snickered. "I'm kinda partial to dogs myself, ma'am," he said. Looking at Brett, he asked, "His name is Mutt?"

"Yeah." Brett nodded.

"What kind of dog is he?"

"Mutt."

Dave laughed. "That's the best kind."

As if he understood Dave's words, the sad-eyed dog moved to his chair and looked up at him, wagging his bushy tail. Dave cleared his throat, threw a timorous glance at Dottie, then said to the dog, "I would slip you some, Mutt, but the lady of the house might let us both go hungry."

Dottie laughed. Mutt settled on the floor beside Dave. From time to time the tall man furtively let his hand dangle beside his chair. Mutt gratefully and quietly received juicy morsels from the generous stranger.

While he and Mutt enjoyed the meal, Dave complimented the Barrigans on their beautiful home. It was expensively furnished and decorated. He was fascinated by the way it had been constructed on a steep slope, actually wedged into the side of the mountain, overlooking Georgetown from the south. It was a virtual fortress, nestled in among towering cedar, spruce, and pine trees.

Also discussed at the meal was the fight in which Dave had participated. Mrs. Barrigan and Emily expressed interest in Christopher John's welfare. In the course of the discussion Dave learned that Merilee John was the Barrigans' part-time maid and that Chris was the Barrigan Mining Company's bookkeeper and payroll clerk.

Brett was all eyes and ears, and it was evident he admired the man who everyone thought was Dan Starr. When the conversation lulled momentarily, the youth said, "Mr. Starr, I wish I could have seen the fight today. Did you really knock Fred Lobdell out with one punch?"

Dave cleared his throat. "Well, I guess so. But I took him partly by surprise."

"And you coldcocked Leonard Whaley, too?"

Dave chuckled. "Yeah, Brett. But it took a little longer with him."

Eyes wide, Brett said, "Would you teach me how to fight?"

Dave cast a wary glance at Dottie Barrigan, then said, "Best way to learn to fight . . . is to fight. Fellow will pick it up fast when he has to."

"But isn't that a little rough on your face?"

"Uh-huh. But a few loose teeth and a bloody nose or two will do wonders to prod a man into being tough. However, if we get a chance while I'm in Georgetown, I'll see if I can give you a few pointers."

"Great!" exclaimed Brett, his eyes lighting up. "Then I want you to teach me how to fast-draw! I really—"

"Hold on, Brett," interrupted his father. "I don't mind Dan teaching you some fisti-cuffs, but guns are out."

"Your father's right, Brett," Dave spoke up. "If you never strap a gun on, you'll never have to pull it."

"Speaking about your being in George-town, Dan," said Morey Barrigan, "did you find anything in that stack of wanted post-ers?"

"Sure did," replied the blond man, thinking guiltily of his own hand-drawn images. "I was a little shocked to find out I had killed two of the infamous Curwood broth-ers."

"*Curwood?*" exclaimed Derek Sheffield. "You mean the Kansas Curwoods?"

"Yep," said Dave, swinging his gaze

on the Barrigans' son-in-law. "Older one was Brant. Kid was named Jake."

"There's a whole bunch of brothers in that family, isn't there?" queried Brett.

"Uh-huh," said Dave. "Started out with nine. All outlaws since Quantrill's raid. Hard to say how many are still alive, but . . . whatever the number was at this time last night, there are two less now."

"You find a poster on the other one, Dan?" asked the senior Barrigan.

"No, sir," responded Dave. "Just the two Curwoods."

"Bounty on the Curwoods, of course."

"Yes, sir. Two thousand each."

Barrigan smiled. "Good! I suppose we contact a federal office in Kansas?"

"Topeka. U.S. marshal."

"All right. As chairman of the town council I'll make the contact for you, since we don't have a marshal. The U.S. marshal at Topeka is a friend of mine, name of Jim Stokes. It'll probably take about three weeks to get approval for Carl Anderson to draw you up a draft at the bank. Can you hang around that long?"

"For four thousand dollars I can hang around that long," said Dave levelly.

III

Emily noticed Dave Bradford's coffee cup was empty. She excused herself and hurried to the kitchen, returning with a steaming coffeepot. Without asking, she gracefully re-filled his cup.

"Thank you, Miss Barrigan," Dave smiled.

Emily returned the smile, then answered him in what sounded like perfect French. While she filled cups around the table, each time responding in French, Dave studied her pretty face. When she sat back down, he said, "I take it you are studying French."

"Not really," said Emily. "Just enough for my lines in the play."

"Emily aspires to be an actress, Dan," said Morey Barrigan. "She finished school last spring. A month or so later she learned through a friend that a new play was in production over in Central City . . . at the Opera House. The girl who was to act the part of a French maid took sick, and they were looking for another girl to take her place."

"So Daddy drove me over," chimed in Emily excitedly, "and I got the part."

"Well, that's wonderful," said Dave, patting Mutt's head.

Emily glanced across the table at her mother, a trace of sadness touching the young woman's dark brown eyes. "Everybody's happy about my getting the part except Mother," she said plaintively.

Dottie Barrigan held her daughter's gaze for a moment, then looked at Dave. "I'm just not sure I want that kind of life for Emily, Mr. Starr," she said quietly. "Besides, I'm not convinced that she has acting ability. Even Emily doesn't know."

"Oh, but I *do*, Mother," Emily said defensively. "I have the talent. I just know I do!"

Dave was not sure of what to say, so he innocently asked, "When does the play open?"

"In two months," replied Emily. "I'm working on my lines now . . . and practicing my accent. A month from now we start working together. The whole cast, I mean."

"That's one of my objections," spoke up Dottie. "Emily will be living away from home. She'll be staying in one of those hotels in Central City."

Emily laughed, throwing a glance at her father. Then looking at Dave, she said, "I'll be staying in a room with three other girls, Mr. Starr. Daddy thinks it's all right. Mother objects."

"Well, Sis," put in Brett, "once you prove to Mom that you have acting talent, she'll give in to the rest of it."

"I'll do just that," replied Emily. Casting an appealing look toward Dottie Barrigan, she added, "That is, if Mother comes to see the play."

"Now, honey," said Dottie, "you know I'll come." Reaching across the table and squeezing Emily's hand, she said tenderly, "I just want what's best for you."

Her daughter squeezed back, smiling. "I know you do, Mother."

"Well," said Dave, standing, "these old bones are tired. Think I'll meander on down to the marshal's office and turn in."

The big dog, tail in motion, looked up at his newfound friend.

"The offer of a soft bed right here still stands, Dan," said Morey Barrigan.

"I appreciate that, sir," Dan said with a smile, "but I'll rest better down there on the cot. I'd take Mutt along, but I wouldn't want him to miss his own dinner."

The tall man thanked Dottie Barrigan for the excellent meal, bid the family good night, and stepped out into the darkness. The mountain air was crisp. A stiff breeze rustled the treetops as Dave moved out of the dark forest that surrounded the Barrigan house. Descending the steep grade, following the vague outline of the wagon ruts, Dave looked up at the moonless expanse overhead. There was something majestic about these Colorado Rockies—the roaring of the river far below; the wind in the giant trees, stirring the air with the sweet smell of pine and cedar; the ragged, towering peaks, silhouetted against the black, star-spangled sky.

"Exhilarating!" Dave said to himself. A man could live all his life in these magnificent mountains and never miss the rest of the world.

Reaching the bottom of the grade, he crossed the bridge over the swift-moving river and soon found himself strolling up the town's main street. The tented saloons were dark, but up ahead the Red Rose and the Big Buffalo were well-lighted and filled the night air with familiar saloon sounds.

Dave walked the middle of the street as he passed the Big Buffalo. Miners and cowboys staggered along the boardwalks. As he came abreast of the Red Rose the music and talk abruptly stopped, replaced by sudden, ominous silence. In a saloon that usually meant one thing—a shoot-out was impending.

Curiosity aroused, the man wearing tied-down twin Colts stepped onto the boardwalk and slowly approached the swinging doors. Peering through the blue haze of the smoke-filled saloon, Dave saw the hulking back of Frederick Lobdell. He was standing next to the long mahogany bar, his big frame trembling. Facing Lobdell at the other end of the bar was a young, slender, hatchet-faced man who had the cut of a gunslinger. He was standing spread-legged, his right hand hovering over the low-slung, tied-down revolver.

The crowd was pressing away from the two men. One of the saloon girls was weeping. Bradford saw Leonard Whaley, his face pulpy, leaning awkwardly against a table. Fear lined his swollen features.

Lobdell's gun hung loosely at his side. He kept his trembling hands at chest level, making it obvious that he was not going to reach for the gun.

"Draw!" bellowed the gunslinger.

Lobdell was shaking his ponderous head. "I . . . I ain't n-no gunfighter," he stammered. Drops of sweat beaded up on his forehead. "I'll fist fight yuh, Manford, but I ain't no gunnie."

Cautiously, Dave palmed open the louvered doors. Their squeaky sound magnified the silence in the room.

The slender gunslinger's dark, piercing eyes flicked to the door and settled on the tall, imposing figure. Dave moved forward and stood beside Lobdell. The quivering man glanced nervously at him out of the corner of his eye, afraid to take his gaze off his challenger.

The young gunslinger regarded Dave with icy contempt. "Butt out, mister!" he snapped. "This ain't none of your affair!"

Holding the slender man with his own cold glare, Dave spoke in quiet voice to Lobdell. "I seem to remember telling you to get your carcass out of Georgetown."

With quivering lip, Lobdell said, "Well . . . I, uh . . ."

"If you want to see the sunrise tomorrow, you'd best take Leonard over there and do as I told you."

Manford bared his teeth. "He ain't goin' anywhere, mister tall man, till he draws on me. Now you just butt out. Unless you want to face me first. Then you can be at hell's gates to meet this big fat slob. He'll be right behind you."

The whimpering, painted woman spoke up. "Please, Jerry. Please. Freddie was just funning. He wasn't really trying to take me away from you."

"Shut up!" snapped Manford, without looking at her. "Now you draw, Lobdell!"

Lobdell's breathing came in short gasps.

"Get out, Lobdell," said Dave evenly. "Right now. I mean out of town. For good."

The huge man hesitated, eyes still fixed on the vicious gunman. Jerry Manford was like a rattlesnake. Lobdell was afraid to move for fear he would strike.

Dave's pale blue stare fixed on Manford as he barked, "Right now, Lobdell!"

The big man abruptly wheeled and dashed out through the door. Leonard Whaley followed on his heels.

With a glint of malice in his dark eyes Jerry Manford said, "That little deed is gonna cost you your life, mister tall man."

"Better back off, Manford!" came a male voice from the crowd. "That ain't no greenhorn you're dealin' with. That's Dan Starr himself!"

Manford's mouth twitched perceptibly and his eyes widened. Then a wicked sneer curled his upper lip. "Dan Starr, eh? I heard that you were up in these parts. Tell you what. Jerry Manford will just show the world who's the fastest right now." Eyes widening farther, he growled, "Draw, Starr!"

Holding his gaze steady, Dave said, "You're the challenger, sonny. Hop to it." Dave's hand hung tensely over the well-worn grips of his twin .45s.

Still sneering, Manford goaded, "Age before beauty."

Without hesitation, Dave quipped, "Dirt before the broom."

Manford's angry hand snaked downward.

The invisible hands of Dave Bradford were suddenly filled with roaring Colts. Jerry Manford died on the floor of the Red Rose Saloon, his hand clutching the revolver still tight in its holster.

Quietly, the tall, blond man dropped the weapons in leather and strode to the door. He disappeared into the darkness, leaving gun smoke to mingle with tobacco smoke.

At sunrise Dave rolled off the cot in the marshal's office. He borrowed the dead lawman's razor and shaved with cold water, used his comb to arrange his thick blond locks, then donned his flat-crowned Stetson and moved out into the nippy morning air.

The miners were hustling off to work in clusters of three and four as Dave walked across the street toward the Alpine Café. The sweet aroma of hot coffee and frying bacon met his nostrils as he stepped into the café. Patrons smiled at him as he paused at the door, searching for an empty table.

A familiar voice called out from the table in a far corner. "Mr. Starr! Over here!" It was Christopher John. Motioning, the young bookkeeper said, "Come sit with us!"

Merilee John smiled up at the tall man as he weaved among the tables and drew near. "Good morning," she said cheerfully.

"Morning, ma'am," Dave said, removing his hat.

Chris shook Dave's hand. "Sit down, Mr. Starr. Merilee and I allow ourselves the luxury of one breakfast out a week. We'll buy yours this morning too."

"Oh, no, you won't," came a feminine voice from behind. "I'm buying Dan's breakfast this morning."

Jo-Beth Taylor held a steaming coffeepot. She was wearing a fresh gingham dress that perfectly complemented her figure.

"I'm not entirely destitute of funds," said the man posing as Dan Starr, though in truth he virtually was. "Nobody needs to pay for my breakfast."

"I'm taking care of it," said Jo-Beth emphatically. "I've had a crush on this handsome fellow here for about nine years, and I reserve the right to buy his first breakfast in Georgetown." She took his hat and hung it on a nearby rack.

Dave's face flushed as he eased into a chair. Pouring his coffee, the pert blonde said, "Chris and Merilee have already ordered, Dan. How would you like to have the same kind of breakfast Mom used to make for you in Amarillo?"

"Uh . . . yeah. Yeah, that'd be just great." He nodded.

"Coming up," said Jo-Beth. "One Mom Taylor Amarillo special!"

With that she was gone. Dave smiled and wagged his head as he watched her move toward the kitchen. Somehow Jo-Beth Taylor did not belong in a hot, stuffy little café in Georgetown, Colorado. She had genuine class. Though she did a lot for the gingham, she belonged in silk and lace, Dave thought. She carried herself like a born and bred lady—a lady of society and refinement. What was she doing here?

Chris's voice intruded into Dave's thoughts. "We heard about the shoot-out at the Rose last night, Mr. Starr. Alf Boggs said Manford went for his gun first . . . and never got it out of the holster. You really that fast?"

"Naw," said Dave, blowing over his steaming coffee. "Manford was just a little slow."

"That's not the way Alf tells it," spoke up Merilee. "Manford was known to be one of the fastest around, Alf said."

"Well, we all have our off days," Dave commented dryly.

"Manford will never have another off day," said Chris.

Dave raised his eyebrows, then nodded. Changing the subject, he said, "How's your ribs, by the way?"

"Pretty sore," admitted Chris. "Like I've been kicked by a mule."

"I want to thank you again, Mr. Starr," said Merilee, "for helping my husband yesterday."

"Couldn't stand by when things got lopsided," said Dave. "I think Chris would've

48

whipped Lobdell if that other fellow hadn't butted in."

Jo-Beth came up behind Dave's shoulder. As she unloaded plates from a large tray and set them before the young couple, she said, "Yours will be ready in about five minutes, Dan."

"If it goes any longer," quipped Dave, "just drag my starving corpse out the back way."

Jo-Beth rapped him lightly on the head with the empty tray and bounded for the kitchen.

"Do you mind if we go ahead and eat, Mr. Starr?" asked Chris. "Merilee is due at the Barrigan house at seven o'clock."

"Oh, of course," said the blond man, "go right ahead. Wouldn't want to make anyone late for work. Besides, cold breakfast is as dull as last week's newspaper."

Dave looked up to see two neatly dressed men standing over him. "Pardon us for intruding, Mr. Starr," said one, "but we just wanted to thank you for stepping in to help Chris yesterday . . . and for ridding this town of the likes of Jerry Manford." Extending his hand, he added, "I'm Vernon Doss. I run the Doss Hardware and Gun

Shop. This here's Mac Fischer. Owns the Fischer Feed Company."

Dave shook hands with both men, accepted their heaping praise humbly, and tried to pass it off as something any man would do.

"Few men can handle themselves like you do," argued Doss.

"Right," agreed Fischer. "If we had more men like you in this world, we'd all be better off."

Conscience-smitten, Dave wondered what these kind gentlemen would say if they knew he was an outlaw with a price on his head.

"Well," said Doss, "we're off to an early council meeting this morning. Morey Barrigan frowns on tardiness. See you later."

The two businessmen filed past the tables and out the door. A few seconds later Jo-Beth reappeared with a heavily loaded food tray. Merilee gasped, Chris smiled, and Dave swallowed hard, as Jo-Beth placed two stacks of pancakes, a plate of steak and eggs, and a half-dozen biscuits plus butter, syrup, and strawberry jelly on the table.

"Hey," laughed Bradford, "I'm not a plow horse!"

Hands on hips, Jo-Beth said, "That's what Mom used to fix for you. Remember?"

"Oh. Sure. Sure," Dave lied. "Who could forget it?"

"You're not slipping, are you?" asked Jo-Beth, devilment in her sky-blue eyes.

Dave cleared his throat. "Oh . . . no, ma'am."

"Then dig in," she said firmly. "I'll be back to pick up all the *empty* dishes later."

Dave shook his head as Jo-Beth whisked away. Then, picking up knife and fork, he dug in.

Thirty minutes later the young blonde came out of the kitchen, followed by a small, serious-looking Chinaman wearing an apron and carrying a carving knife in his hand. Obviously he was the cook. Leading him up to Dave's table, she said mirthfully, "Now, that's a good boy, Dan! You ate it all up. You want some more?"

"Uh . . . no, ma'am," said Dave, standing up and laying a hand on his full stomach. "I've had quite enough, thank you."

Jo-Beth laughed. Turning to the Chinaman, she said, "Tinky, I want you to meet an old friend of mine. Mr. Dan Starr."

The curious little man stepped forward. Dave started to extend his hand, but the Chinaman, ignoring the gesture, put his heels together, folded his arms, and bowed from the waist. "Velly glad to meet you, Mista Starr," he said.

Clumsily imitating the Oriental bow, the long-bodied Texan said, "Me, too, Mr. Tinky."

The pint-sized cook disappeared into the kitchen.

"Tinky, huh?" said Dave, smiling.

Jo-Beth broke into a healthy laugh. "Actually we call him that because we can't pronounce his real name. He got tired of trying to get us to say it right."

Dave chuckled at that, and after fetching his hat and thanking Jo-Beth for the meal, he left the café. As he did, he saw Morey Barrigan standing in the doorway of the Georgetown Bank with Carl Anderson, Vernon Doss, and Mac Fischer. Barrigan detached himself from the others and moved in his direction. "Oh, Dan!" he called. "May I have a word with you?"

Dave stopped and waited for the mine-owner to catch up to him.

"If you don't mind," Barrigan said. "I'd like a word with you. Can I buy you a drink over at the Big Buffalo?"

"Don't think I could swallow my saliva, sir," said Dave. "That Jo-Beth filled me with so much food and coffee, I can hardly move."

"Well, what do you say we go over to the marshal's office then?"

"All right," replied Dave.

As they walked together, a buckboard passed. "Mornin', Mr. Starr," said the driver, waving.

"You've become a celebrity here, Dan," said the mineowner. "That's part of what I want to talk about."

Both men touched their hat brims as a pair of women met them on the boardwalk in front of the office door. "Good morning, Mr. Starr," they said in unison. "Nice day," added one.

"Sure is, ladies," said the imposter.

When they were in the office, Morey Barrigan closed the door. "Dan," he said, "I'll get right to the point."

Dave sat on a corner of the desk and looked at Barrigan, waiting.

"I just came from a town council meeting," said the distinguished-looking man. "We had a unanimous agreement that I should approach you about hiring on as the marshal of Georgetown."

The outlaw blood in Dave's veins turned cold. "Oh, I couldn't do that, sir," he said quickly. "I've got to hit the trail just as soon as I get my four thousand dollars."

"But you're perfect for the job," argued Barrigan. "You've demonstrated that already. You whipped Fred Lobdell and his partner, ran them out of town. You outdrew and killed that Manford fellow. I tell you, Dan, you're just what we need to clean up this town and keep it that way."

Dave shook his head, staring at the floor.

Before he could speak, the chairman of the town council said, "I think you ought to settle down, Dan. Sink your roots, find yourself a good woman, get married, raise a family. Here's your chance to do just that. Why, when word spreads that the famous Dan Starr is marshal of Georgetown, the no-goods and the gunslicks will make a sharp detour around this place."

Still shaking his head, Dave said, "I'm sorry, Mr. Barrigan, but I'm a drifter. I have to be on the move. I—"

"Even if we double the salary that Marshal Plummer was getting?" butted in Barrigan. "I'd put in the other half personally. We were paying Bo a hundred a month, plus room and meals. How's two hundred sound?"

"That's very generous, sir," said Dave, standing up, "but I just can't do it."

"Well, how about this?" countered Barrigan. "How about taking the job until we can hire a permanent man?"

"I can't obligate myself to an indefinite period, sir," Dave equivocated. "You might be a long time getting a new man."

"Not with two hundred a month dangling in front of their eyes."

"You're really going to pay that much?"

"For the right man."

Dave knew there were good lawmen working for less than half that amount. Once word was out, Georgetown would have a dozen men to pick from within a few days. He took a deep breath, pursed his lips, and let it out slowly. "Okay, Mr. Barrigan. I'll wear the badge until you get a new marshal . . . *or* until my bounty comes through. Whenever that happens, I'll be on my way."

Barrigan smiled and shook Dave's hand. "Good!"

"By the way," Dave said, "did you wire the U.S. marshal in Topeka about my money?"

"Yes, sir," said the mineowner. "Did that while you were stuffing yourself at the Alpine. Asked my friend Stokes to handle it personally." Barrigan fingered his mustache. "Come to think of it, I'm going to wire Jim Stokes again. He has contact with a lot of lawmen. He'll find us a man right away."

"Sounds good," said Dave.

"Okay," said Barrigan, "as chairman of the town council, I need to swear you in. Raise your right hand."

Dave slid off the desk, stood to full height, and hoisted his right hand.

In a serious tone the chairman of the town council said, "Do you swear to uphold the laws of the United States, of the State of Colorado, and of the town of Georgetown, and to enforce them to the best of your ability?"

"I do," came Dave's response. He felt like a blatant hypocrite.

"Fine," said Barrigan. "You'll find a badge in the top drawer on the left side of the desk. You already have a key to the office. The keys to the cell doors are in the top drawer on the right side. As of now you are on the town payroll. Charge your meals at the Alpine. Georgetown will pick up the tab."

Heading for the door, Barrigan paused and said, "Oh, just a couple other things."

"Yes?"

"If you have to use your gun, replace the bullets at Doss's gunshop and charge them to the town. The other thing is, you don't need to call me Mr. Barrigan. Just make it Morey."

"Okay, Morey." Dave smiled.

"And one other thing . . ."

"Yes?"

"You're invited to dinner at our house again tonight. We'll celebrate your becoming interim marshal."

"It's a deal," said the blond man. "I'll never pass up that kind of cooking."

As Morey Barrigan made his way to the Western Union office he passed the word to no fewer than a dozen people that Dan Starr was the new marshal of Georgetown. He had just reached the telegraph office when the door opened and Derek Sheffield came through it. Sheffield's pale features whitened as his eyes focused on the face of his employer. "Oh, hello, Dad," he breathed weakly. "I . . . uh . . . sent off the wire to the bank in Kansas City yesterday. Stopped in to see if they'd sent an answer."

Barrigan wondered why his son-in-law seemed so fidgety. "And?"

"The payroll money will be on the trail to Denver on the seventeenth."

"Fine." The mineowner nodded. "Say, you might like to know that Dan Starr is our new marshal."

"Oh, really?" said Sheffield. "Boy, that's, uh . . . that's really great, Dad. Town ought to be safe now."

"That's the way I feel about it too," said Barrigan, nodding.

"See you at the office, Dad," Sheffield said, hurrying down the street.

Again Barrigan wondered at his son-in-law's nervousness, but quickly passed it off. "Howdy, Clarence," he said, entering the Western Union office.

Clarence Sheets, a skinny little man in his late sixties, looked up from under his green-shaded visor and said, "Howdy, Mr. Barrigan. What can I do for you?"

"Want to send a wire to Topeka, to Jim Stokes."

Dave Bradford hiked the steep slope to the Barrigan house as darkness was descending on the Colorado mountains. As he drew near the house he heard the warning bark of the big dog. Suddenly Mutt bounded off the porch, barking like a wild beast. The moment he recognized his tall friend, he stopped barking and stood on his hind legs, panting.

"Hello, Mutt," Dave greeted him, leaning over to rub the furry neck.

Morey Barrigan was on the porch, smiling. "Looks like you've found a friend, Dan," he said with a chuckle.

"Yes." Dottie nodded from the open door. "And I know why."

Evasively Dave said, "It's my magnetic personality."

"Personality, my eyes," retaliated Dottie. "It was your sneaky left hand!"

The Barrigans laughed, and Dave joined in as they passed through the door, Mutt included.

Emily and Brett were in the dining room. Congratulations were offered to Dave on his new position as marshal of Georgetown. The elder Barrigan eyed his son-in-law's empty chair and said, "I don't know what's keeping Derek. We'd best go ahead and eat."

As the diners settled in their chairs Dave said, "I saw Derek go into the telegraph office when I left the hotel to come up here."

"Is that so?" said Barrigan. "Wonder what he was going in there for? He already got his message from Kansas City about the payroll money."

While the assembled company began to eat, Barrigan explained to Dave that he had cash for three months' payroll sent in four times a year from a large bank in Kansas City. It amounted to just over a hundred thousand dollars. There were no banks in Denver that could supply the currency for even a month's payroll, so it had to be done this way.

The money was transported under heavy guard by rail to Denver, then brought by coach to Georgetown, where it was locked in a heavy-duty safe at the mine office. Transportation dates were staggered at the end of each quarter, to ward off robbers.

Mutt was pressing his nose into Dave's hand below the table when Derek Sheffield walked in. "Sorry I'm late," he said apologetically. "I got tied up at the office."

"You mean the telegraph office?" queried Barrigan.

Sheffield seemed momentarily taken aback, but then he said smoothly, "No. Clarence had asked me earlier in the day to pick up some chewing tobacco for him. He had some important messages coming in and couldn't leave the office. I took it by and was ready to come up here when one of the miners came running to me. Said someone wanted to see me over at the office. Trivial matter, but it took time nonetheless."

Sheffield began shoveling mashed potatoes onto his plate, and a bit nervously he said to the big blond man, "I hear you're our new marshal, Mr. Starr. Congratulations."

IV

Actually, the reason Derek Sheffield had been in the Western Union office earlier in the day had nothing to do with bringing Clarence Sheets more chewing tobacco. Nor did it have anything to do with seeing if the bank in Kansas City had wired back about the payroll shipment. Indeed, as Morey Barrigan had stated, Sheffield had already learned the exact date of the shipment. The real reason the red-haired man had waited until dusk, then quickly slipped into the telegraph office, had been totally different.

As Sheffield had closed the door behind him, Clarence Sheets had looked up.

"Got to send another wire, quick, Clarence," said the nervous Sheffield. Pulling a folded piece of paper from his shirt pocket, he slid it across the counter.

The old man's weathered brow knotted. "How much longer do I have to keep this up?"

"Just a couple more weeks or so," Sheffield said with false assurance.

"If I get caught sending messages without keeping copies, I'll lose my job," said Sheets plaintively. "I ain't gittin' no younger."

"Isn't a thousand dollars worth the risk?" asked Sheffield.

"I ain't seen none of it yet," complained the old man.

"You will, when this whole job is wrapped up. Now get this on the wire, quick."

"How much is the telegraph operator in Lawrence gittin' for keepin' his mouth shut?" demanded Sheets, curtly.

"I don't know what Curwood is paying him," snapped Derek, "but it's not as much as you're getting. Now you just put it on the wire."

Suddenly the telegraph apparatus began to click.

"Excuse me a minute," said the old man. Quickly he grabbed a pencil and began to write the message as the clicker sang out the Morse code.

Turning toward the door, Sheffield said, "I'll see you later. You get that message off to Curwood."

"Hold it, Derek," snapped Sheets. "This wire is for you."

Sheffield turned back slowly. "Curwood?"

The old man nodded as he wrote. When the clicker stopped, he scribbled for a few seconds, then handed the paper to the anxious young man.

Sheffield snatched it quickly and read it. A humorless smile twisted his lips. "Good!" he exclaimed. Handing it back, he said, "Burn this."

Clarence Sheets watched Sheffield disappear through the door, then sat down at the desk. Wadding up the paper, he laid it in an ashtray, struck a match, and set it on fire. While wisps of smoke sailed upward, he put his finger to the telegraph key and tapped out the message Sheffield had given him a few moments before.

ADAM CURWOOD
LAWRENCE, KANSAS
MAN WHO KILLED YOUR BROTHERS HAS BECOME MARSHAL OF GEORGETOWN. REPEAT

AS IN LAST MESSAGE. NAME IS DAN STARR.

D.S.

Adam Curwood stood in the Western Union office in Lawrence, Kansas, his face florid with rage. He swore a violent oath. Slamming the counter with a powerful fist, he said, "So Dan Starr is Georgetown's new marshal, huh? He killed Brant and my little brother Jake. Mr. Starr doesn't know it, but he's a dead man!"

Crumpling up the message just handed him by the telegraph operator, Curwood swore again.

Horace Bailey trembled and said, "Is th-there anything else I can d-do for you, M-Mr. Curwood?"

"Yeah," said Curwood, heatedly. "Send a message to Sheffield and thank him for the information. Tell him I'll be waiting for the date of the payroll shipment."

"Y-yes, sir."

"And Horace . . ."

"Yes, sir?"

"Tell him I'll take care of Marshal Dan Starr."

A warm glow of satisfaction flowed through Derek Sheffield as he climbed the steep grade toward the Barrigan house. Lady Luck had sure smiled down on him. How fortunate that just five days ago his old friend Tom Dart had ridden into town with Brant Curwood's bunch.

In a private conversation over a few drinks, Derek and Tom had talked of old times in Kansas City when the two boys used to steal things together. Laughing, they recalled how they "put it over" on storekeepers. They reminisced over loot shared and enjoyed, and Tom playfully chided Sheffield for having met Shirley Barrigan and given up the life of petty crime. Tom, of course, had later been caught and sent to reform school.

Sheffield had lost track of him since then, but two years later young Dart had been released and subsequently taken up a life of crime. He had been in Leavenworth Prison twice in the past eight years and now was making it big robbing banks with Brant Curwood's gang.

Tom had introduced Sheffield to the Curwood brothers, Brant and Jake, behind closed doors. Perhaps Tom had sensed that larceny was still in Sheffield's blood. Trusting his old friend, Tom had shared with him the gang's plans to rob the Georgetown

Bank. They asked Sheffield if he knew when the bank might have a good supply of cash.

As business manager of the Barrigan Mining Company, Sheffield was aware of the town's financial matters. Nearly everybody in Georgetown worked at the mine. Payday came on the first of the month. This was May thirtieth. Sheffield suggested the gang rob the bank just before closing time on June second, which would give the miners time to spend their money in the stores and saloons. The merchants would put their deposits in the bank at the close of the biggest business day of the month.

Brant Curwood was overjoyed at the information. He would cut Sheffield in on the take.

As the conversation and drinking proceeded, one thing led to another. Soon Sheffield spilled the anger bottled up inside him. His father-in-law was getting filthy rich on the mine, and Sheffield was held to a set salary. It was a substantial salary, but not enough to satisfy the ambition and greed that seethed inside him. He wanted more. Much more.

He had been the one to introduce the subject of the payroll shipment. Upon learning the details of how the money was shipped from Kansas City, Brant Curwood had put Sheffield in contact with his notorious older brother, Adam. Buying off telegraph operators in Georgetown and Lawrence, Adam and Sheffield set up plans. Adam and his gang would intercept the train west of Topeka.

Sheffield would get a twenty-five percent cut of the loot for setting it up. Adam Curwood would wait for Sheffield to wire the date of the shipment. Morey Barrigan always set the date himself, staggering it for safety's sake. When his decision was made, he would tell it to his business manager, who would handle sending the wire to the Kansas City bank.

Sheffield smiled to himself as he neared the dense trees that circled the big house. The latest message from Adam Curwood confirmed that the gang would be ready for the train on June seventeenth. Curwood expressed his appreciation for Sheffield's naming the man who had killed Brant and Jake, and promised him a bonus for the information.

Sheffield looked at the yellow light shining through the windows of the house and chuckled again. His bonus might even fatten a little more for the information he had just sent to Adam Curwood. Now the outlaws would know exactly where to find Dan Starr. Since he had taken the job as marshal, Starr would be in Georgetown.

One cold thought shafted through Sheffield's mind as he mounted the porch of the house. He must plan carefully and fake a way to suddenly come into all that money. Shirley must never know how he got it. Sheffield loved his wife passionately. He wouldn't be able to stand losing her. And then there was Timmy and the precious baby girl. Nothing must ever happen to take them away from him. It already worried him half to death that they might be returning from Kansas City on the same train that carried the company payroll.

Moving through the door, Sheffield passed into the dining room, where the Barrigan family and the new marshal were eating.

Sheffield made an excuse for being late, saying that he had been tied up at the office. He was surprised when his father-in-law queried him about being at the telegraph office. Sheffield's heart leaped with fear. Someone must have seen him going into the Western Union office and conveyed the message to Barrigan. It must have been the new marshal.

Forcing a mask of calm, Sheffield lied his way out of it. During the rest of the meal he tried to busy himself with his food and let the others do the talking. But he did not have much of an appetite.

It was late in the evening when Dave Bradford bid the Barrigans and their son-in-law good night. He thanked Dottie for the meal and stepped out into the darkness, picking his way down the steep trail. At the base of the slope he crossed the bridge and turned onto Georgetown's main street. The stores and shops were dark. Only the two saloons, the hotel, and the Alpine Café were open.

Dave walked along, checking the doors, making sure they were locked. He finished one side of the first block, then crossed the street and did the same thing on the other side.

Moving into the second block, he rattled doorknobs until he came to the door of the Western Union office. It was dark inside, and he was puzzled when he turned the knob and the door opened. Since many of the merchants lived in apartments on the second floor, over their places of business, he stepped off the board sidewalk and moved into the street where he could see above the wooden awning that extended over the office door. There was light in the window above.

Stepping back to the door, Dave knocked loudly on the jamb. Presently a shaft of light hit the back wall of the office. An elderly man with a lighted cigar in his mouth came down the rickety stairs, bearing a lantern. The strong odor of the cigar instantly filled the room. Lifting the lantern high, he squinted toward the tall, shadowed figure that filled the doorway.

"Yes?" said Clarence Sheets.

"I'm the new marshal, sir," came the voice of the obscure figure. "I was just checking doors along the street. Found this one unlocked."

"Oh, thank you, Marshal Starr," said Sheets, moving toward him. "I guess I'm gittin' forgetful in my old age." He extended his right hand. "I'm Clarence Sheets."

"Glad to meet you," said Dave, the cigar smoke burning his eyes.

As the tall man blinked, Sheets jerked the cigar from his mouth and said, "Oh, excuse me, Marshal. I only smoke these things when I'm up in my room."

"You just *chew* when you're down here, huh?" Dave chuckled.

Sheets cocked his head. "Chew? You mean terbaccy, Marshal?"

"Yeah."

"Never chewed terbaccy in my whole dad-burned life, Marshal. What made you think I chewed?"

"Oh . . . uh, I guess I just assumed it," said Dave. "Glad to have met you, Mr. Sheets. I'll be on my way now. Lock your door behind me."

"You bet, Marshal," said the old man. "G'night . . . and thanks."

Dave pondered Derek Sheffield's lie about taking chewing tobacco to the telegraph operator, and his nervousness at the supper table. He continued his task, passing the noisy Red Rose and the Georgetown Hotel. He moved on to the third and final block of business establishments, then crossed the street and started back in the other direction. The only place with any lights in the third block was the Alpine Café.

Just as Dave reached the café the lights went out and the door came open. Jo-Beth

Taylor appeared, looking through the gloom at the tall man. "Oh, hello, *Marshal Starr*," she said warmly. "Congratulations. It's sure going to be a comfort having you to watch over our town."

"Well, it's only until Morey Barrigan can find a permanent man," said Dave.

"Oh?" said the young woman, with a note of disappointment. "I thought it *was* permanent. I wonder why Mr. Barrigan didn't tell folks that."

"I guess he's got a good reason," remarked the man who posed as Dan Starr.

Behind Jo-Beth the little Chinese cook came through the door, rattling the lock with the key. Turning, he peered at Dave and said, "Ah, Marshal Starr. Velly glad to see you this evening."

Dave bowed to match Tinky's bow.

"I'm just walking my rounds," Dave said to Jo-Beth. "Making sure the town is tucked in for the night."

"Tinky always sees me home," said the young woman. "Won't let me walk alone."

"That's good," said Dave. "Would Tinky trust me to walk you home this time?" The words had passed his lips without forethought. *Why did you say that, Bradford?* he asked himself.

The Chinaman bobbed his head. "I will trust you, Mister Starr." He grinned. Looking at the woman, he said, "Good night, Miss Taylor. I will see you in the morning."

"Good night, Tinky," said Jo-Beth, touching his arm. "See you in the morning."

The little Chinaman hustled away, turned the corner, and was gone.

Offering Jo-Beth his arm, Dave said, "I need to check the next block on this side and stick my head in both saloons. Then we'll get you home."

Jo-Beth nodded.

As they moved forward he said, "Come to think of it, I don't even know where you live."

"I have a small house down by the river," she replied. "Not far from the bridge."

Dave finished checking the doors, then left Jo-Beth on the boardwalk while he stepped into the Big Buffalo. His appearance was greeted with applause and congratulations. The bartender assured him all was quiet, and Dave returned to Jo-Beth.

"Now the Rose," he said, leading her across the street.

Music from a tinkling piano rang out in the air as Jo-Beth waited for the tall man to return. There were voices carrying on a conversation, but she could not distinguish what was being said. This time it was taking longer. Curious, Jo-Beth Taylor inched up to the door and peered inside.

Dan Starr was talking to Mac Fischer at a table about midway in the room. One of the saloon girls was hanging on a husky miner at the end of the bar, near the door. She rolled her painted eyes at Jo-Beth and said in a catty tone, "Why don't you come on in, honey? We won't contaminate you!"

Jo-Beth blushed and quickly stepped away from the door. The girl and the miner guffawed.

Outside Jo-Beth stood with her back to the wall, breathing hard. She wished Dan would hurry. Suddenly the swinging doors squeaked and the husky miner stepped out. Moving close to her, he said, "Come on inside, girlie. I'll buy you a drink and you can join in the fun."

"No, thank you," said the young blonde, her blue eyes suddenly angry. "I don't drink."

The big, smelly man moved closer. Jo-Beth wanted to run away, but didn't.

"No time like now to start," said the miner, placing his palms on the wall on each side of her. Putting his face close to hers, he breathed, "You're a pretty little thing." His breath was foul.

Turning her head, she said, "Get away from me."

"Aw, now, darlin'," said the miner, "you and I need to get acquainted. My name's Sam Penno. What's yours? I'm new here."

"I'm not your darlin'," snapped Jo-Beth. "Now get away from me!"

Leaning closer, Penno said with whiskey-foul breath, "How's about a little kiss for Sam, honey? I bet you'd like it."

Before Jo-Beth could speak again, Dave Bradford's sharp voice said, "Back off, mister!"

Palms still pressed against the wall, Penno turned his head slowly, let his eyes rest for a moment on the shiny badge, then looked into the angular face of the marshal. "Just havin' me a little fun with the missy, Marshal," he said in an innocent tone. "Ain't breakin' no law."

"I didn't ask what you were doing, bub. I told you to back off."

Penno straightened up. His face went dark. "You take off that badge, pal," he growled, "and we'll see if I have to back off."

"You've already been told that you have

to," rasped Dave. "I'm in no mood for a smart mouth. Just go on back inside and be a good boy."

Jo-Beth slipped down the boardwalk, sensing what was coming. Dave saw it in Penno's dark eyes just before the man swung his meaty fist.

Penno lunged. Dave sidestepped, whipped out his right-hand revolver, and brought the barrel down savagely on the miner's bushy head. Penno collapsed in a heap. Faces appeared in the doorway. Dropping the .45 into its holster, Dave said, "Couple of you men drag this body to wherever he's staying. He'll sleep well now."

As the tall man gave the young woman his arm and guided her up the street, he said, "Sorry, Jo-Beth."

"It's not your fault, Dan," she replied, squeezing his arm. "He probably wouldn't have harmed me. But his breath would kill an elephant."

Dave laughed. "You're some gal, Miss Taylor."

Five minutes brought the couple to the west end of town, where Jo-Beth's little house stood by the rippling river. The clouds overhead, which had covered the moon since dusk, parted, and the night was sprayed with silver light.

As they drew near the house the lovely young woman said, "Let's look at the moon in the water."

Without speaking, Dave allowed Jo-Beth to guide him to the bank of the river at the rear of the house.

"Oh, look, Dan!" she exclaimed. "Isn't it beautiful?"

"Sure is," agreed the imposter, looking into the swirling water.

Jo-Beth Taylor took a deep breath and exhaled, saying, "Ahh! Isn't it just heavenly? I love these mountains, Dan. Sure is prettier country than the flats of the Texas panhandle."

"Uh-huh," agreed Dave. He was silent for a long moment while they watched the swift water, then said, "Jo-Beth, what brought you to Georgetown? Why are you here, living all alone?"

Without moving her eyes from the silver-coated water, Jo-Beth Taylor said pensively, "I came here three years ago to get married. His name was Chad Waxman."

Quietly, Dave asked, "What happened?"

"I met Chad in Pampa. Little town northeast of Amarillo."

Dave waited for her to go on.

"My parents were killed in a tornado when I was sixteen, and I went to live with my aunt in Pampa. Chad was passing through on his way to Colorado. He was coming here to open a café. Georgetown was booming because of the gold strike. Chad's grandfather had left him some money, and he felt a café would be a sound investment."

"Makes sense."

"We fell in love," said Jo-Beth. "At least I thought we did. Chad said he'd go on to Georgetown and get the café started. I was to follow in six months. We would be married when I got here."

"And?"

"I came. But Chad had fallen in love with Carla Anderson, the banker's daughter. They ran off together, got married, and are living in Denver."

"Oh."

"A wire came two days after I arrived here. My aunt had died. I had nowhere to go. Mr. Anderson felt bad for the way Chad had treated me. Chad had sold the café to Mr. Anderson, so he needed a manager. I got the job."

"I'm glad that worked out for you," said Dave.

She shrugged. "Mr. Anderson pays me well and even gives me a percentage of the profits. I couldn't do this well anywhere else. I love it here, except . . . except . . ."

"You're lonely," said Dave flatly.

Jo-Beth's eyes misted. She nodded, looking back at the rushing river.

"I know the feeling," said Dave huskily.

The couple stood looking at the river. Nothing was said for several moments. Then Jo-Beth turned toward the towering figure who stood over her. Moonlight glistened in her eyes. Dan could not help himself. He folded the captivating young woman in his muscular arms and kissed her tenderly.

On June 16 Adam Curwood paced the floor of an old abandoned farmhouse five miles south of Lawrence. It was nearly sundown, and the gang had not shown up yet. They were already an hour overdue.

While he paced, the elder Curwood cursed the name of Dan Starr. Six of the Curwood brothers had died in various ways in the past four years. Darrell and Chuck had been hanged in Oklahoma for murder. Earl was killed in a barroom brawl. Gabe was gunned down in Hays, Kansas, and Frank in Joplin, Missouri. Harley had been poisoned by a woman he had jilted.

The only remaining brothers Adam had had left were the second oldest and the youngest of the brood. Then Brant and Jake had been shot and killed by Dan Starr. Derek Sheffield's wire had said that Jake tried to give up, but Starr had shot him between the eyes in cold blood.

Thirty-eight-year-old Adam was all alone now. Hatred for Marshal Dan Starr boiled inside him like a seething volcano. Starr was going to die. And Adam Curwood would find a way to make him sweat before he killed him.

The last of the Curwoods stood two inches under six feet tall and was a hefty one hundred eighty pounds. There was a touch of gray in his temples, sideburns, and mustache. His dark, curly hair was kept neat and well-trimmed. In a business suit he would be taken for a lawyer, a banker . . . or even a well-dressed lawman.

Hearing hoofbeats drumming on the hard earth, Curwood stepped to the door. There they were—nine of the most ferocious renegades who ever turned sour on society. They lived to rob, plunder, steal, and loot. Anyone who stood in their way would die in a hail of gunfire.

Adam Curwood's chosen first lieutenant was Norm Woodman. He was clever and cunning, and his specialty was robbing trains. Next in line was Tony Musio. Slick, heartless, and ambitious, he had spent nearly half of his thirty-odd years of life in jail.

Curwood eyed them as they dismounted in a cloud of dust. Miles Frazier and Al Craig looked as if they had used their faces as battering rams. Curwood snapped, "You boys been scrapping?"

Norm Woodman spoke up for them. "They got into a little ruckus with some cowpokes at the Sunflower Saloon."

Shaking his head, the gang's boss said, "I hope those cowpokes look as bad as you boys. They certainly couldn't look any worse." Turning to Woodman, he said, "I take it this is why you're late."

Norm nodded. "Yeah. Sorry."

"Take your horses around back, boys," Curwood said to the group. "Then come on inside. We got things to talk about."

The sun dipped below the western edge of the flat Kansas prairie as the motley gang gathered inside the farmhouse and sat in the semicircle on battered chairs and boxes. Norm Woodman situated himself in the middle. Flanking him on the left were Mike Poston, Nelson Blechman, Al Craig, and D.J. Salem. On his right were Tony Musio, Jim Hicks, Miles Frazier, and Hutch Reiner.

Adam Curwood seated himself in an old rocking chair, propped his right foot on his left knee, and ran his gaze over the scabby, bearded faces. The only one with a shave and a decent haircut was Tony Musio. Tony was dark and extremely handsome. He wore thin sideburns down to his earlobes and a mustache to match. He had a mean, crafty look in his black eyes.

"Got a wire yesterday afternoon, boys," began Curwood. "The Barrigan payroll will be on the next train, on the seventeenth."

"Hey, that's tomorrow!" spoke up Al Craig.

Curwood nodded. "We'll have to roll out of here early in the morning, get ourselves positioned at the spot we talked about on the other side of Topeka. The payroll will be quite sizable. This ought to be a haul you can tell your grandkids about."

Wicked smiles captured the outlaw faces.

"As usual," continued Curwood, "we don't touch the moneybags until we bring the loot back here. Norm and I will count it and divvy up the shares. Of course, whatever we take off the passengers we also divide among us."

Details were discussed for several minutes, then Tony Musio said, "What about this bird who murdered your brothers? You gonna let us help you track him down?"

"Won't be necessary," Curwood said with hatred in his steel-gray eyes. "Got a wire after the one about Brant and Jake being killed that I haven't told you about."

"Oh, yeah?"

"Yeah. Dan Starr has hired on as marshal of Georgetown. He'll be a cinch to find. So after we get back here with the loot, I'm heading for Colorado. I'm going to see that murdering snake dead. And I want to pull the trigger myself."

After his men had gone, Curwood thought about Dan Starr. A wicked sneer curled his mouth. "I'm going to make him sweat before I kill him," he said audibly to himself. "I haven't figured how yet, but Mr. Starr is going to have a few sleepless nights before I show up in Georgetown and blast his guts out. I want him to think about it for a while first."

Adam Curwood lay in his bed that night and worked out his diabolical plan to murder the man he thought was Dan Starr. Long after midnight the scheme came together in his mind. Satisfied that vengeance would be his, he drifted off to sleep.

After breakfast at a Lawrence café Curwood ambled down the dusty street to the local undertaking parlor. A faded sign over the door stated that the mortician's name was Arnold Isman. A tiny bell rang over his head as Curwood entered the establishment. Footsteps sounded from the rear of the building. Presently a small man in his middle fifties, wearing half-moon spectacles, pushed his way past the deep-purple curtains that covered the doorway to the front office.

"May I help you, sir?" asked the little man. Doing a double take, he said, "Oh. I know you. You're one of the Curwood brothers. Let's see," he went on, raising a finger to his mouth. "I know you're not the youngest . . . uh, Jacob. And I don't think you're Brant. But what is your first name, Mr. Curwood?"

"Adam," said Curwood flatly. "Brant and Jacob are dead."

"Oh, dear," said the undertaker, eyes

widening. "And you are here to make arrangements for their funerals."

"Nope. They were buried in Colorado," responded the outlaw dryly. "I want to buy a coffin."

Arnold Isman's eyes took on a blank look. "You, uh . . . what?"

"I want to buy a coffin," repeated Curwood. "Want to play a little joke on an old friend."

"Oh. I see. A joke?"

"Yep. You got a plain pine coffin?"

"Yes, sir."

"How much?"

"Thirty dollars, Mr. Curwood," said Isman, working up a smile.

"Okay," said the outlaw. Adjusting his gun belt, he asked, "How much to paint it for me?"

"Excuse me, sir?" said the little man, tilting his head and looking at Curwood over his spectacles. "Did you say you want the coffin *painted?*"

"Yeah. Black."

"Black?"

"Yeah. I want you to use the kind of paint that goes on stovepipes. I want it to be dismal and dull, and as black as the inside of a panther's belly. Okay?"

"Uh . . . yes, sir. Whatever you say, Mr. Curwood."

"How much altogether?"

"Well, it will probably take a couple of coats of regular black paint, then a couple coats of the stovepipe."

"I want the inside black, too, Mr. Isman," said Curwood. "Even the underside of the lid."

"Oh. The inside. Well, in that case . . . I would say, with the labor, it will cost an additional ten dollars. Forty, total."

"Fine," said the outlaw. "You want some money on it now?"

"No, sir. You can pay me when it's done."

"How soon can I get it?"

"Would day after tomorrow be all right?" asked the little man.

"No. I have to have it by sundown tomorrow. I'm putting it on the night train to Denver."

"Oh, my," said Isman, adjusting his spectacles. "That is going to be a problem. I don't know if—"

"How about if I add a twenty-dollar bonus for getting it done by the time I need it?" cut in Curwood.

The undertaker cleared his throat. "Well, I think I could manage to . . . uh—"

"Fine." The outlaw smiled. "And by the way, Mr. Isman, this little transaction is just between you and me. Okay? If anyone else found out about it, the joke would be ruined. Understand?"

"Yes, sir." The little man nodded and winked. "Wouldn't want to ruin a good joke!"

V

On the morning of June 17 Dave Bradford signed the meal ticket at the Alpine Café. Handing it to Jo-Beth behind the counter, he said, "Tell Tinky I said the breakfast was scrumptious."

She smiled and said, "I'll tell him."

Dave looked into her eyes, then forced himself to turn toward the door. He said, "See you later, Jo-Beth."

"Later," echoed the captivating woman.

Dave reprimanded himself for the deep feelings he was having for Jo-Beth Taylor. He felt he had no right to involve her in his life, that he was living a lie right in front of her. The warmth and affection she was giving were not his to take since she thought he was Dan Starr.

Making his way up the wagon-rutted street toward the cutoff that led to the mine office, Dave reminded himself that he would be leaving Georgetown as soon as his money came through. He must not allow himself to get any more involved with the beautiful Jo-Beth.

Something else lay heavy on Dave's mind as the Barrigan office came into view: Derek Sheffield's lie about taking chewing tobacco to Clarence Sheets. It really was no big thing, yet suspicions kept nagging at him. There was a huge shipment of money coming from Kansas City. It would involve Morey Barrigan setting the date for the shipment . . . and Derek Sheffield wiring the Kansas City bank.

Dave decided he should talk to Barrigan about it. He wouldn't accuse Sheffield, just tell Barrigan he had a hunch and ask him to change the shipment date.

Derek Sheffield was immersed in paperwork as Dave entered the office. He looked up and said, "Morning, Marshal Starr."

"Morning, Derek." Dave smiled. "I understand your wife and children will be coming home soon."

"That's right," replied Sheffield.

"Bet you're excited, huh?"

"Sure am."

Craning his neck toward the inner office, Dave said, "Mr. Barrigan in?"

"Yes." Sheffield nodded. "Dottie's with him at the moment, but you can go on in."

Dave knocked on the door of the inner office and Morey called out for him to enter.

Dottie invited him for dinner the next night, explaining that their daughter Shirley and the two grandchildren were due in on the stagecoach tomorrow afternoon. The dinner was a welcome home for them.

Dave began to refuse the invitation, not wanting to intrude on a family affair. But when Dottie told him that Jo-Beth Taylor was coming, Dave weakened and changed his mind. Dottie explained that Shirley and Jo-Beth were best friends.

Kissing her husband's cheek, Dottie Barrigan left the office, closing the door behind her.

Morey Barrigan gestured toward a chair in front of his desk. "Sit down, Dan," he said. "I assume you came to talk to me?"

"Yes."

"Before you do," said Barrigan, "I have some good news for you."

"Oh?"

Easing back in his chair, Barrigan said, "Got a wire from Jim Stokes in Topeka. Our new permanent marshal will be here within a few days."

"Who's the new man?" Dave asked.

"His name's Todd Daley. He's been marshal in St. Joseph, Missouri, for several years, been wanting to move to Colorado. He'll come first and his wife'll follow later, to give him a little time to find a house."

"Well, that's good," commented Dave. "Do you have an exact date when he'll arrive?"

"No. Naturally, he has some loose ends to wrap up, so it'll be a few days yet. Your bounty money ought to be processed about the time he gets here."

"That's good," said Dave. A cold thought seized his mind: *What if Daley recognizes my face from a wanted poster?*

"Now," said Barrigan, "what did you want to see me about?"

Dave fingered his hat, turning it in his hands. Looking the mineowner straight in the eye, he said, "You'll probably think I've lost my marbles, Morey. But I've got a feeling down in my stomach about your payroll."

Barrigan's brow furrowed. "What do you mean?"

"I can't really put it into words," said Dave, "but I've got this gut feeling that you ought to change the date of the shipment from Kansas City."

Barrigan's face stiffened. "You know something I don't?"

"No," responded Dave. "It isn't something I know. It's just something I feel."

Barrigan studied Dave's angular face. "Gut feeling, huh?"

"Yes, sir."

"Okay. We'll delay it a few days. There's a lot of money at stake. If I didn't follow your hunch and the train got robbed in spite of the guards, I'd kick myself from here to the Kansas line." Wiping a hand over his mouth, he said, "Four days sound all right? I can still have it here in plenty of time for Chris John to prepare the payroll."

"Yes, sir," said Dave. "Four days would make me feel better."

Dave left the office and walked down the street. He stepped between two buildings and faded into the shadows. He was positioned so he could watch the front door of the Barrigan Mining Company office.

In less than five minutes Derek Sheffield

came out and made a hurried beeline for the Western Union office. Dave thought he detected nervousness in the young man's features, and his suspicions were reignited.

He pondered the situation. If he was right in his assumption that Sheffield was setting up a robbery, the red-haired man would have to wire his accomplice of the date change. Even if he could not wire the new date until the Kansas City bank had confirmed it, he would have to contact the accomplice immediately in order to stop the robbers from hitting the wrong train. It would be leaving Kansas City in about seven hours.

Dave knew that the telegraph operator would have to be working with Sheffield in order to accomplish the plot. But asking Clarence Sheets any pointed questions would lead nowhere. Clarence could deny it, and Dave could prove nothing. Dave had to laugh at his own position. Usually he was the man *planning* the robbery. How strange instead to be wearing a badge on his chest . . . and being the man trying to foil it!

Dave let Sheffield get inside the telegraph office, then moved out of the shadows and hastened down the boardwalk. Reaching the door, he turned the knob and casually entered. Sheffield was writing a message on the Western Union form. He twisted around to see who had come through the door, using his sleeve to wipe away the moisture on his brow. "Oh. Howdy, Marshal," he said. Dave noticed he did not try to hide the message he was writing.

"Howdy, Derek," Dave responded. His gaze moved to Clarence Sheets's nervous eyes. "Morning, Clarence," he said, smiling.

"Nice day, Marshal Starr," said Sheets, forcing a smile. "What can I do for you?"

"I'm expecting a very important wire from the new marshal who's coming to Georgetown," Dave lied. "Anything come in?"

"Not a thing, Marshal," said Sheets.

Eyeing the red-haired man once more, Dave said, "You look worried, Derek. Anything wrong?"

Sheffield again mopped his brow with his shirt-sleeve. "Wrong? Not at all," he said, trying to keep his voice steady. "My . . . my father-in-law just decided to change the date of the payroll shipment from Kansas City. I have to hurry and get the message to them. It's scheduled to be put on the train this afternoon."

Dave nodded. "Go right ahead. Don't let me stop you."

Sheffield finished scratching the message. Dave knew that if his hunch was right, Sheffield would need to send a second wire in a hurry.

Shoving the paper across the counter, Sheffield said, "Hustle, Clarence."

As the elderly man took the paper and sat down at the desk, the sweaty business manager of the Barrigan Mining Company eyed Dave shakily. "Really, Marshal, there's nothing wrong. I guess I just appeared upset because I was in a hurry to get this message to Kansas City."

"Oh. Sure," said Dave. "I can see why you'd be wanting to get that right on the wire."

Sheets tapped out the dispatch. Sheffield waited, hoping the man he knew as Dan Starr would leave. Dave leaned on the counter, conveying that he was staying.

"Okay, Derek," said Sheets. "I'll let you know when your reply comes in. Probably be late this afternoon or tomorrow mornin'."

Sheffield rubbed his nose and said, "Maybe it'll come back right away. I think I'll just wait around."

Sheffield's insides were churning like

a windmill in a hurricane—he had to get word to Adam Curwood immediately. If Curwood's men proceeded with the robbery, it could jeopardize the chances of ever pulling it off in the future. Once Curwood's men stopped that train and demanded the Barrigan payroll, Morey Barrigan would make drastic changes. This was a once-in-a-lifetime opportunity.

Sheffield's face paled when Dave said, "Tell you what, Derek. The message I'm expecting is quite important. I'll have to wait right here till it comes. If yours comes in, I'll send somebody over to the office to tell you." Derek Sheffield's blood went cold.

Adam Curwood stood in the back room of Arnold Isman's undertaking parlor and looked over the black coffin. A smile spread across his face. "Perfect, Mr. Isman," he said emphatically. "Just perfect."

"I'm glad you're satisfied, Mr. Curwood," replied the little man.

"Now I'd like to ask one more thing of you, sir," said the outlaw. "For another twenty dollars would you deliver it within the hour to the depot and see that it gets on the train?"

Isman arched his eyebrows. "Guess I can't refuse, can I?"

"Good," said Curwood, peeling four twenty-dollar bills from a thick wad. "Now in order for this joke to work, Mr. Isman, you must never tell *anybody* who bought the coffin from you. Understand?"

"Yes, sir." Isman bobbed his head.

"If anybody ever inquires about it, the man who bought it told you his name was John Doe, okay? You never saw him before. And you sent it on the train in that name too, okay?"

"Yes, sir," said the undertaker.

"Here's another twenty to pay for shipping it by stagecoach to Georgetown. Won't cost quite that much. You keep the difference."

"Thank you, Mr. Curwood."

The outlaw reached in his coat pocket and produced a white envelope. "I want you to nail the lid down after I put this envelope inside." Then, pulling a tag from another pocket, he said, "Attach this to the outside."

"I'll take care of it, Mr. Curwood," Arnold Isman said with assurance.

Adam Curwood laughed to himself as he walked away from the undertaking parlor. *Wish I could see Starr's face when his coffin*

96

arrives, he thought. *You just sweat it out for a little while, Mr. Starr. You murdered Brant and my baby brother. I'm going to kill you and then bury you in that black box!*

Curwood had not decided how he would kill the man he thought was Dan Starr. But he would find a way to make him stare death in the face before he died.

Moving down the street, Curwood felt the wind pelt his face with tiny drops of rain. In the murky sky above, black cumulus thunderheads were boiling—much like the hatred that seethed inside him. The man who had murdered Brant Curwood and shot Jake Curwood between the eyes was going to feel the force of their big brother's wrath.

Thunder followed lightning across the turbulent night sky. The big engine barreled its way through a driving rain, sending the mournful cry of its whistle across the Kansas flats. The dark, brooding night seemed to close in around the thundering train like a black shroud.

Behind the hissing behemoth of steel followed the coal car, the baggage coach, three passenger cars, and the caboose. Squared shafts of yellow light bit into the darkness through the windows while passengers occupied themselves in various ways. The steady clickety-clack of the wheels filtered its way into the cars.

In the first car, on a seat near the front, a young mother cradled a small baby while trying to keep her five-year-old son from annoying those around him. Directly across the aisle sat a middle-aged beak-nosed spinster who glared at the tow-headed boy, annoyed at the restless youngster.

"Mummy," said the boy, while twisting in the seat, "are we almost there?"

Shirley Sheffield's face pinched in frustration as she replied through tight lips, "No, Timmy. I told you we won't be in Denver until tomorrow. Don't you remember? We only left Kansas City when the sun was going down."

"But I'm tired of this old train," complained Timmy, his lower lip protruding. "I want off." As he said that, the boy threw his cap across the narrow aisle, striking the already irritated spinster in the face.

The woman snapped her head around as she grasped the cap. Her eyes were as hard and brittle as glass. With voice to match, she flared, "I'll be *glad* to help you off the train, little boy! In fact, if you don't sit still and shut your mouth, I'm going to *throw* you off!"

Shirley opened her mouth to retaliate, but held her peace as Timmy coiled up next to her, plainly frightened. His body and mouth were frozen stiff, eyes bulging.

Farther back in the car an elderly couple was chattering excitedly about seeing their grandchildren in Denver. Across the aisle sat a prosperous-looking man reading a Kansas City newspaper. Others in the car studied the raindrops that beat against the windows. In the last seat a man who had boarded a half hour earlier at Topeka snoozed.

Things were much the same in the second passenger coach.

In the third car two cowboys slept in the first seats, which faced backward, their hats tilted over their faces. Across the aisle and three rows back a poker game was in progress. The coach was filled with a pall of blue smoke from the four cigars in the mouths of the gamblers. Two upended suitcases served as the table.

Periodically some of the cards would slide to the floor as the coach swayed and rocked. The gamblers kept a whiskey bottle moving among them. The more they drank, the more boisterous they became. They laughed, spoke loudly to one another, and swore vociferously.

A skinny little man in his late seventies was sitting behind the clamorous gamblers, next to his wife, who was disturbed by their profanity. She eyed them with distaste. Now and then the cowboys in the front of the smoke-filled car lifted their hats and peered pugnaciously at the noisy foursome.

The elderly man finally got his fill and stood up in the aisle. Moving to the gamblers, he steadied himself against the sway and said, "Gentlemen, I would like to bring to your attention that there are ladies present, and one of them is my wife."

"Well, don't complain to me, grandpa," said one of the gamblers in a thick drawl. "You married her!"

The others laughed hoarsely.

"Gentlemen," said the old man, "I'm asking you to refrain from swearing in my wife's presence."

"Yeah, and quiet down while you're at it!" came an unidentified male voice from the rear of the coach.

One of the gamblers, a ruddy-faced man with slicked-back hair, guffawed and blew cigar smoke at the old man.

He ignored it. "It it doesn't stop," warned the old man, "I will speak to the conductor!"

The red-faced gambler eyed the left hand of the elderly complainer, which gripped the wicker seat. He casually pressed the hot tip of his cigar against the flesh. The little man howled and jerked his hand away. At the same moment the coach lurched and the old gentleman fell to the floor. A man leaped from his seat to assist him while the poker players laughed heartily. One of the cowboys raised his hat from his face and glared heatedly at the gamblers again. He was just starting to get up when the conductor came through the door from the second car.

The conductor's face stiffened under the dark-blue cap he wore. "What happened?" he asked as the elderly man gained his feet and eyed the burn spot on his wrinkled hand.

"This man burned him with his cigar," volunteered the passenger who had helped the old man from the floor.

The accused gambler swore and said, "It was an accident, Conductor, I—"

"Accident, nothin'!" snapped the old man, rubbing his burned hand. "You did that on purpose!" Turning to the conductor he said, "I asked these men to quit using profanity with ladies present."

The conductor set a pair of stern eyes on the four offenders. "You gentlemen will refrain from using foul language while on this train."

"Tell them to quiet down too!" came the unidentified voice from the rear of the coach again.

The ruddy-faced gambler slammed his cards down and swore vehemently. Jumping up, he poked a stiff finger against the conductor's chest and hissed around his cigar, "We'll talk like we want to, shorty. You hear me? We bought tickets on this train, and we'll say what we want to say as *loud* as we please. Got it?"

The conductor blinked and said, "I . . . I'll have to put you off this train!"

The ruddy man laughed wickedly. "And just who you gonna get to do that?"

The dry, double click of a hammer being thumbed back came at the same instant the gambler felt cold metal against the nape of his neck. "I'll handle it," said the tall cowboy.

The gambler froze.

"You boys are disturbin' my sleep with

your racket," drawled the cowboy. "Now, let's put the cards away and let people rest."

A second gambler stood up, anger in his dark eyes. "Now, look here, cowman," he said through his teeth, "you ain't tellin' us we gotta quit pl—"

The cowboy's fist lashed out, connecting squarely on the man's nose. He went down in a heap, blood oozing from his nostrils. The other two gamblers jumped to their feet, their eyes flashing fire.

Turning to his partner, the cowboy said, "Rex, get the cards."

As Rex leaned over and confiscated the deck one of the other gamblers jutted his jaw belligerently and rasped, "I'm gonna get you, cowboy!"

The cold muzzle was removed from the first gambler's neck long enough to slam down on the temple of the threatening man. He slumped back into his seat, dazed. The red-faced one snaked his hand inside his coat and produced a derringer. The irate cowboy cracked the gambler's wrist with his gun barrel. The derringer clattered to the floor as the stricken man howled.

"Conductor," said the cowboy, while ramming his muzzle into the gambler's belly, "stop the train. These buzzards are gettin' off."

The conductor nodded with a victorious grin and headed out the front door of the coach.

"Now, look, mister," spoke up the fourth gambler, "you can't do this!"

"Just watch me," said the cowboy. He held the muzzle tight against the first gambler's stomach and said, "Let's move toward the front."

The train started to slow down as two of the gamblers helped their friend with the purple temple to his feet. The cowboy called Red moved ahead and opened the door. As the steel wheels ground to a halt the conductor appeared through the back door of the second coach. The triumphant smile was still on his face.

"Out!" snapped the cowboy, his gun now pressing the red-faced gambler's spine.

The prairie wind lashed rain between the cars as the gamblers were forced off the train into the darkness. "I'm gonna sue this railroad!" bellowed the one with the bloody nose. The foursome huddled together beside the track.

The conductor swung a lantern for the engineer to see, and the train lurched forward. The ruddy-faced gambler bared his teeth in the dim light and snarled, "We'll meet again, cowboy! And when we do, you're a dead man!"

The slender cowboy tipped his hat with a caustic smile as the train pulled away. The four gamblers were last seen standing in the wind and rain as the caboose passed them by.

Returning to the car, the conductor closed the door and extended a wet hand to the cowboy. "Thanks a lot, mister," he said with a toothy grin, "Sorry, I don't know your name. Mine's Lum Smith."

"Name's Art Landis," said the cowboy, holstering his gun. "This here's Rex Tomlinson."

"Sure do appreciate your help," said the conductor, shaking Tomlinson's hand. "We got some coffee brewed in the baggage coach. Would you gents like to move up with me for a little sip?"

Landis and Tomlinson accepted. After being thanked by the passengers in the third coach, the cowboys followed Lum Smith through the other cars.

The baggage car was dimly lit by a lone lantern that hung on a hook next to an old pot-bellied stove. Fire flickered inside the stove. A soot-blackened coffeepot danced on its top.

Four wooden chairs sat next to the stove in a semicircle. The conductor motioned toward the chairs. "Drop your carcasses in there, boys, an' I'll pour."

Smith filled tin cups with the dark, steaming liquid and handed them to the cowboys. Pouring another for himself, he sat down and blew on the hot contents. Art Landis let his eyes roam through the coach. Along one side was a rack containing luggage of various shapes and sizes. At the end of the car were several wooden crates, stacked to the ceiling.

Then he saw it.

Resting on top of four wooden crates next to the large sliding door was a long black coffin. It was made of pine, but had been painted a deep, dull black. The sliding door was open about six inches to let some of the heat from the stove escape. Rain was splattering the floor around the opening. There was a white paper tag attached to one end of the gruesome box. The tag fluttered in the wind.

Rex Tomlinson was eyeing the strange black coffin also, when Landis spoke.

"When'd they start paintin' coffins black, Lum?"

"Dunno," replied the conductor, sipping coffee. "First one I ever saw. I've seen some metal ones used by rich folks that were painted gray. But I've never seen a *black* coffin before."

"Someone shippin' a corpse west, huh?" said Tomlinson.

Smith threw a leery glance at the black box. "Don't rightly know. Somethin' strange."

"What do you mean?" queried Landis.

"Well," answered the conductor, "we took it on back at Lawrence. But two men loaded it easily by themselves. I watched them. Didn't appear to be very heavy."

"You mean it's empty?" asked Landis, standing up.

"Dunno," replied Smith. "I ain't touched it."

The tall, lanky cowboy stepped to the black coffin and rapped his knuckles on the side, then the top, then the side again. Each time, it gave off a hollow sound. Under the watchful eyes of Smith and Tomlinson, Landis shook his head and rapped again. Moving to the end of the oblong box, he slipped his fingers underneath and hoisted it upward.

Easing it back down, Landis said, "I'd swear it's empty." He raised his Stetson and scratched his head. "Why would anyone send an empty pine coffin out west? There's plenty of pine out there." With evident curiosity he fingered the fluttering tag and angled it toward the pale yellow light so that the three men could read it:

> Marshal Dan Starr
> Georgetown, Colorado,
> to be opened
> ONLY
> by addressee

"Dan Starr?" exclaimed Tomlinson. "It couldn't be *the* Dan Starr."

"You mean the gunfighter?" queried Lum Smith.

"Yeah." Tomlinson nodded. Taking a gulp of coffee and swallowing carefully, he added, "Georgetown's havin' a big gold boom, I hear. Guess they'd need a gunhawk like Starr to handle things."

"Probably so," agreed Landis.

"I talked to a fella once," put in Smith. "Said he'd seen Dan Starr in a shoot-out against three top drawer professionals. Happened over in Abilene. Said them two .45s plumb jumped outta their holsters. Starr tattooed his initials on each one's chest before they could clear leather!"

Landis swung his gaze back to the somber coffin. "Why would somebody send Starr a coffin? And why paint it black?"

"There's no indication on the tag as to who sent it?" asked Tomlinson.

"Nope."

"There'd be a name on the shipping sheet," said Smith, standing up and walking to a tattered file cabinet. Pulling open a drawer at the top, he produced a worn folder. Flipping it open, he stepped under the light. The desired sheet was right on top. It was dated June 17, 1873. He read it quickly, then chuckled.

"Well?" said Landis anxiously.

"Sender's name was John Doe," Smith said dryly.

The train threw sparks and smoke toward the ebony sky as it continued westward, cutting its way through the driving rain.

In the cab the engineer said to the fireman, "Bob, you want to sit in for me awhile? Eyes are smarting."

"Sure," agreed fireman Bob Warner. "Why don't you slip back to the baggage coach and get some of Lum's coffee while it's hot?"

Engineer Ralph Moore rubbed his eyes and lowered himself from the high seat. He watched as Warner boosted himself into the padded leather chair and laid his hand on the throttle. Moore wheeled and was gone.

Bob Warner leaned out the window and squinted at the wide yellow circle painted on the night by the powerful mirrored headlight. The slanting sheets of wind-driven rain made a glaring silver wall against the beam. The glistening parallel tracks of steel seemed to end a hundred feet ahead.

Twenty minutes passed, then something caught the fireman's eye in the darkness up ahead. Orange sheets of flame reached skyward in the center of the track. Warner blinked his eyes, rubbed them, and peered through the rain again. Now, in addition to the fire, he saw swinging lanterns on both sides of the track. Fearful, the fireman eased back the big throttle and wished for Ralph Moore.

In the baggage coach the engineer was discussing the black coffin with Lum Smith and the two cowboys when the train started slowing down. Moore eyed Smith and lowered his coffee cup. "Something's wrong, Lum," he said, shaking his head. Then the wheels bit into the tracks and the train thundered to a screeching halt.

Suddenly the big door slid back loudly, revealing four men behind drawn guns. Their faces were covered up to the eyes with bandannas, hats pulled low and collars high on their glistening slickers.

"Hands up!" barked one of the robbers as they piled inside the baggage coach.

Meanwhile four other robbers had dashed into the passenger cars, waving their guns and giving orders. They would relieve the passengers of wallets, purses, and jewelry. One other bandit held Bob Warner at gunpoint in the cab of the big engine. Raindrops struck the hot smokestack, giving off little hissing sounds as horses nickered out in the wet darkness where a lone rider waited and watched.

The four masked men relieved Art Landis and Rex Tomlinson of their guns.

"Line up and turn around!" snapped one of the outlaws at the two cowboys and Ralph Moore. "Put your hands on the luggage rack!"

The three men complied, Landis eyeing the man with open contempt.

"Just you pull somethin', cowpoke," growled the outlaw. "It'll give me an excuse to plug you!"

Another robber, who seemed to be in charge, said curtly to Lum Smith, "Where is it?"

Lum's trembling hands remained at shoulder level as he turned around. He spoke timorously. "Wh-where's what?"

"Don't play games with me," the outlaw said in a level tone. "We want the Barrigan payroll and we want it now!"

Smith's face went white. "It—it ain't on this train, mister," he said, running his words together.

The robber swore. Placing his gun muzzle against the man's belly, he said, "Give me the money now, or you die!"

"It's not comin' till later!" blurted Smith. "Don't you think if we had it, the train would be heavily guarded?"

The outlaw glared at the conductor, the words slowly sinking into his brain.

"That may be a trick to throw us off!" spoke up another robber. "Let's break open all the luggage and those wooden crates."

"Good idea," agreed another.

Immediately the four outlaws began their search, scattering the contents of suitcases and boxes all over the coach. When nothing turned up, the outlaw in charge swung his gaze to the black coffin. Pointing with his gun, he said, "Look, boys! Mebbe somebody's pullin' a cute one on us!"

"You mean . . . that coffin?" asked one.

"Yep," said the leader, holstering his revolver and stepping to the coffin. "There a corpse in here?"

"N-no, but—"

Whirling, the outlaw eyed Lum Smith menacingly. "If you lied to me, mister, I'm gonna kill you!"

"Th-there ain't no money in there!" gasped Lum defensively. "That c-coffin was put on at Lawrence. The Barrigan payroll comes from Kansas City."

"You got a claw hammer?" demanded the outlaw.

Nervously, Lum Smith rummaged in a metal toolbox and produced the necessary tool. The bandit boss snatched it from his grasp, holstered his gun, and went to work on the lid. One of the gang noticed Art Landis twisting around to look.

"Hey, cowboy!" he snapped. "You turn around!"

113

Landis obeyed, his mind searching for a way to stop the outlaws.

The nails in the coffin lid resisted the intrusion. They popped and squeaked, but finally gave in. The lid came loose. The boss laid the hammer on one of the crates that held the coffin. "Bring that lantern over here," he said, raising the lid.

The bandit leader swore as the light revealed only a white envelope lying in the bottom. He swore again, slamming down the coffin lid.

The brakeman, George Aubrey, had left the caboose when the robbers forced the train to stop. Bearing a double-barreled shotgun, he had dropped to the ground and circled past the fringe of light into the darkness, gradually making his way forward. He could see the robbers inside the passenger cars, waving their guns at the frightened passengers.

Aubrey thumbed the rain from his eyes as he approached the baggage car. He paused for a moment and studied the scene. Four masked men held the engineer, the conductor, and two male passengers at gunpoint. The brakeman decided this was the best place for him to foil the robbery, with four bandits clustered in one spot. One outlaw had holstered his gun in order to use a claw hammer on a long black rectangular box.

Just as the outlaw angrily slammed down the lid, George Aubrey cocked the hammers of the shotgun and jumped into the light beside the baggage coach. "Drop them guns!" he bellowed.

One of the robbers whirled and fired at the brakeman. When the slug hit Aubrey's chest, he jerked and both barrels roared. The outlaw chief took a full charge in the stomach.

While another bandit shot Aubrey again, Art Landis seized the claw hammer and slammed the bandit in the head. Rex Tomlinson jumped in to help. Guns roared in the momentary melee. Bullets chewed into the walls of the railroad car, and some ripped the flesh of the two cowboys. "Let's get out of here!" shouted one of the outlaws.

Within moments thundering hooves faded away into the night. The gun smoke cleared as Lum Smith and Ralph Moore knelt over the lifeless bodies of Art Landis and Rex Tomlinson.

Smith glanced at the leader, who lay on the coach floor. He was dead—blown almost in half. The one Landis had hit with the hammer lay next to him, his skull caved in. George Aubrey was sprawled on the wet ground, the rain pelting his dead face in the dim spray of light.

Ralph Moore stood up, laid his hand on the black coffin for support, and ejected an oath.

Back at the abandoned farmhouse, Adam Curwood stormed and swore as he paced back and forth. He had lost Norm Woodman and Miles Frazier in the robbery, and except for what they had taken from the passengers, they had come up empty. Whenever the payroll *was* sent, Curwood would never get another crack at it. Barrigan would learn of the attempted robbery and change everything.

Curwood swore vehemently. How did it happen? Did Sheffield double-cross him? Or did Barrigan somehow catch wind of the scheme and change the shipment date?

Adam Curwood knew one thing for sure. That payroll had to get to Georgetown sometime soon. If the boys rode hard, they could be in Georgetown to intercept it. He would take tomorrow night's train and get to Denver ahead of them, wait in Denver until the boys got their hands on the payroll, then ride into Georgetown alone to take out his vengeance on Dan Starr.

He explained his plan to the gang, telling them to get some sleep, then to ride out for Colorado. After they had robbed the Barrigan company of the payroll, they were to look him up at the Brown Palace Hotel in Denver. With that he rode home and went to bed.

The sky was clearing when Curwood arose and looked out his bedroom window toward the east. Red clouds banked above the horizon, stained by the rising sun. The thirty-eight-year-old bachelor shaved, and fixed his breakfast.

Lawrence was beginning to come alive when the outlaw strode down the muddy street toward the depot. The air smelled sweet, washed clean by the all-night rain. Moving through the door of the railroad depot, Curwood approached the ticket agent, who stood behind the barred window.

"Morning," said the agent, with a weak smile.

"I'd like a ticket for the night train to Denver," said Curwood. "Want to go tonight."

"I'm afraid that will be impossible, sir,"

said the agent. "The train won't be going to Denver for a few days."

Curwood looked at him in disbelief. "Why not?"

"There's a trestle over the Solomon River about eight miles west of Abilene," said the agent. "Rain last night weakened the moorings when the river flooded. They've got to shore it up before they can run a train over it."

The outlaw swore. "What do you mean by a few days?"

"Wire said three or four."

"Did last night's train to Denver get across before the trestle weakened?"

"Yes, sir. Damage wasn't discovered till about sunrise this mornin'."

Adam Curwood was relieved to know that at least the black coffin was on its way. He studied the situation. Tony and the boys would wait patiently in Georgetown until the payroll showed up. He would just tarry until the trains were rolling again.

VI

The Wells Fargo stagecoach rolled to a stop on Georgetown's dusty street. It was nearly dark, but Shirley Sheffield could make out the form of her husband standing on the boardwalk. "Look, Timmy," she said, pointing out the window, "there's Daddy!"

As the stage driver swung the door open, the little boy jumped out and ran to Derek Sheffield, who scooped the lad up in his arms and moved toward Shirley. They kissed, then Sheffield lovingly hugged his baby daughter.

"You tired, honey?" he asked his wife.

"Very," she answered.

"Your mother has dinner all fixed. We can go up there and eat first, then we'll get you home so you and the kids can get to bed."

"That'll be fine," said Shirley.

Sheffield loaded his family into a wagon and headed for the Barrigan house. While the horses strained against the steep grade, the red-haired young man said, "I certainly did miss you, Shirley."

"I missed you too," she said tenderly.

"How was your trip?" Sheffield waited for Shirley's answer, a cold feeling forming in his chest.

"Going was fine," replied the young mother. "Coming back was not so good."

"Oh?"

"Derek," she said, holding her voice level, "robbers stopped the train between Topeka and Junction City. They . . . they—"

Gripping her arm, he blurted, "Did they harm you?"

"No," said Shirley. "But they were after Daddy's payroll money!"

Sheffield feigned surprise. "Really? Then your dad's hunch was right."

"What do you mean?"

"He told me the other morning that he had a strange feeling about the payroll . . . had me wire Kansas City and delay it four days."

"So that's why it wasn't on the train," she said. "But it was originally to be on last night's train?"

"Yes," said Sheffield.

"How did those outlaws know it, Derek?"

"I have no idea, honey," he lied.

The wagon stopped in front of the house. Morey and Dottie Barrigan were on the porch to greet them, along with Brett, Emily, and Mutt.

Worry plucked at Derek Sheffield's mind. What was Adam Curwood's reaction going to be? The Curwoods were known for being heartless killers. Sheffield hoped that Adam would give him a chance to explain before gunning him down in cold blood.

After the family had hugged and kissed Shirley and the little one, they moved into the house, where Dave Bradford and Jo-Beth sat on the overstuffed sofa. The couple rose to their feet. Jo-Beth hurried to embrace Shirley, then spoke to Timmy and his little sister.

Turning toward the tall blond man, Jo-Beth said, "Shirley, I'd like you to meet Marshal Dan Starr."

"Glad to meet you, Marshal," said Shirley. Her brow knotted. "Did something happen to Bo Plummer?"

"We had a bank robbery," said Jo-Beth. "They killed Marshal Plummer."

"Oh, no," gasped Shirley.

"But Dan here met up with them and killed them all," put in a wide-eyed Brett.

"He did?" said Shirley, looking at the stranger with new respect. Turning toward her father, she said, "Speaking of robberies, Daddy, our train was stopped by bandits a few miles this side of Topeka last night. They demanded your payroll. When the conductor told them it wasn't on the train, they wouldn't believe it. Shooting broke out. The brakeman and two passengers were killed, two of the outlaws also."

Morey Barrigan's face lost its color. He looked first at Dave, then said to his son-in-law, "That hunch was right, Derek. I'm sure glad we changed the date."

"I guess we were lucky," the young man lamely put in, trying to cover his jangled nerves.

"Daddy," said Shirley, a quizzical look on her face, "how could those robbers have known when you were sending the payroll?"

"It's a mystery to me," admitted Barrigan. "But I can guarantee you there will be an investigation."

Derek Sheffield felt his stomach turn over.

Conversation at the meal covered Jo-Beth's long acquaintance with Dan Starr, the new marshal who was on his way, the health of Derek Sheffield's parents . . . and eventually worked its way around to the payroll. Morey Barrigan wondered if Dan Starr knew more than he was telling.

Brett expressed his confidence that if Dan had been on the train, he would have wiped out the whole gang.

Dave was now sure that Derek Sheffield was a traitor to his father-in-law. He pondered what to do about it, while slipping food under the table to a grateful Mutt. Simply to accuse Sheffield before Barrigan would be useless. There was no proof. The young man could plead innocence and say that the leak was at the Kansas City bank. The obvious alternative was to force a confession out of Clarence Sheets. That also might prove difficult. Dave decided he would have to bide his time on nailing Derek. *Dirty skunk*, he thought. *Biting the hand that feeds him.*

While Dave was deep in thought Shirley asked how things were progressing for Emily in her acting career. Emily brought Shirley up to date, expressing her determination to prove to their skeptical mother that she had acting ability.

With everyone full and satisfied, Sheffield took his weary family home, and Dave, after saying his good-nights, walked Jo-Beth to her little house by the river.

Standing by the rushing water, Jo-Beth looked up at him by the light of a half-moon. "I dread for this Marshal Todd Daley to come, Dan," she said with emotion. "I don't want you to leave."

Dave drank in her enthralling beauty, knowing full well what was happening to him. He was falling helplessly in love with

Jo-Beth Taylor. He scorned himself inwardly. This lovely, sweet creature was too good for him. He was an outlaw with a price on his head. One day he would die at the hands of a lawman . . . or while rotting in some prison.

He wished things could be different. He wished he could forsake the outlaw trail, erase it from his life. He wished he could settle down, marry Jo-Beth, and live a normal life. But it could never be. When she found out he was an imposter, she would hate him.

Suddenly she was in his arms, her soft, warm lips on his. Fire burst in his heart and coursed like molten lava through his veins. Jo-Beth wrapped her arms around him, laid her head on his chest, and said softly, "Please, Dan. Please don't go. I want you to stay here with me."

Dave wanted Jo-Beth more than anything he had ever wanted in his life. Yet he knew he must tell her the truth—then leave her forever. It was the right thing to do . . . the only thing to do.

Again their lips blended in a tender kiss. Then it was his own voice saying, "I love you, Jo-Beth. I love you."

"I love you, too, my darling," she cooed.

"I've loved you since I was thirteen. But now I'm *in* love with you. Please . . . don't ever leave me."

Dave's insides churned. That was exactly what he had to do.

Adam Curwood finished packing his small suitcase. Strapping it securely, he walked to the dresser and pulled open a top drawer. From under some cloth articles he produced a .25 caliber derringer. Breaking the action of the shiny nickel-plated weapon, he checked the loads, then snapped it shut and dropped it in his inside coat pocket. Rummaging further in the drawer, the outlaw found a box of .25 caliber bullets, shook a few out in his hand, and slipped them in a side pocket of his coat.

Curwood then lifted the .45 from the holster on his hip and made sure it was fully loaded.

Grasping the suitcase, he left the house and walked the darkening street toward the depot. He was glad the trestle down the line had been repaired. It had taken exactly four days. Now he could be on his way to Denver. By this time tomorrow he would be on a stagecoach heading into Georgetown. Derek Sheffield was going to answer some questions . . . and Marshal Dan Starr was going to die.

As he boarded, Curwood was surprised to see that the train was nearly full. He made his way into the first passenger car behind the baggage coach and found an unoccupied seat next to the window on the right side. Placing the small suitcase in the overhead compartment, he laid his hat on top of it and sat down.

The train pulled out, rumbling westward. In barely more than an hour it chugged to a stop at the Topeka station.

The few seats that were vacated at Topeka began to fill up as a new crop of passengers boarded the train. Curwood was watching some good-byes on the platform through the window when a deep masculine voice said, "Pardon me, sir, is this seat taken?"

Curwood turned to see a tall, slender man of thirty standing in the aisle. A big revolver was on his hip, tied down to his thigh. The top of his hat almost touched the ceiling of the coach. "Uh . . . no," he answered. "Sit down."

"I've been in the car just ahead since Kansas City," said the slender man, sitting down, "but I got off for a few minutes at

126

Topeka to see a friend, and while I was gone someone took my seat. Car's full, so I decided to try in here." Extending his hand in a friendly manner, he said with a smile, "I'm Todd Daley, from St. Joe."

"Jacob Smith," lied Curwood, gripping Daley's hand. "I'm from Lawrence."

"Oh," said Daley, raising his eyebrows. "Were you there when the Quantrill raid took place?"

The mention of Quantrill stirred vile memories in Adam Curwood, but he decided to evade any discussion about it. "No," he lied again. "I haven't lived there that long."

The train lurched and pulled away from the depot.

Curwood looked out the window at the fading lights. His thoughts turned to the upcoming pleasure of killing Dan Starr.

A picture crept into the outlaw's mind: Brant and Jake lying dead on the side of a Colorado mountain. Jake, who had tried to give up, lying with a dark hole between his eyes. Marshal Dan Starr standing over him, smoking gun in his hands. Vengeance would be sweet. Starr would pay. He would pay dearly.

". . . you in?" Todd Daley's words filtered into Curwood's thoughts.

"What's that?" he asked.

"I said, what business are you in?"

"Oh, uh . . . well, I'm sort of between jobs right now," said Curwood, trying to think fast. "I'm, uh, on my way to Georgetown, Colorado. Going to see a man about an office job at the big mine there."

"Really?" said Daley, his face lighting up. "I'm heading for Georgetown too."

"Is that so?" responded the outlaw, trying to appear interested.

"Yep," said the tall man. "I'm going to be the town's new marshal. I'm replacing the famous Dan Starr. He's been filling in since the previous marshal got killed."

Adam Curwood straightened up in the seat. Now he *was* interested. "I heard Starr was marshal there," he said quickly. "Is he staying till you arrive?"

"Well, he might be," answered Daley. "He's got some bounty money coming to him for killing a couple of outlaws before he pinned on the badge. I understand if he gets the money, he'll leave before I get there." Snapping his fingers, Daley said, "Say, come to think of it, the outlaws he killed with money on their heads were from Lawrence.

Curwoods. Brant and Jake Curwood. You know them, Smith?"

Curwood's blood went hot. Covering his wrath, he said, "Uh . . . no. I've seen some of them around town, but I don't know any of them."

The conductor passed through the coach, collecting tickets, then opened the door and disappeared. Daley slid down in the seat and pulled his hat over his face. The car bobbed and weaved to the steady click of the wheels. The passengers were settling down with pillows.

Adam Curwood looked out the window into the darkness and contemplated the situation. Todd Daley was on his way to become the new lawman in Georgetown. Curwood wondered if Daley knew anyone there. Perhaps he had taken the job sight unseen. It would not be the first time a town marshal had been hired that way. If so, lady luck was riding with Curwood . . . and the way had been paved for his smooth, undetected entrance into the Colorado mountain town. He would skip staying in Denver and go straight to Georgetown. He would leave a message at the Brown Palace Hotel in case he missed the gang at Georgetown.

The outlaw leader reached in his shirt

pocket for a cigar, purposely elbowing Daley stiffly. The slender man jerked, lifted his hat, and adjusted himself.

"Sorry," said Curwood. "Didn't mean to wake you up. I was just digging for a cigar. Want one?"

Daley sat up straight and pushed his hat to the back of his head. "No, thanks. Cigarettes are my speed. But now that you mention it, I think I'll roll me one."

While Georgetown's prospective marshal tapped tobacco into the thin paper, Curwood lit up his cigar. Pressing for much-needed information, he asked, "Who hired you in Georgetown? I mean, who'd you deal with?"

Daley ran his tongue along the roll, then replied, "Same man you're going to see about a job. Morey Barrigan. He's chairman of the town council."

"You meet Barrigan somewhere to apply for the job?"

"No," said Daley, striking a match. "I've never met him." Touching the flame to the tip of the cigarette, he added, "I've never been in Georgetown."

Curwood's pulse quickened. "How'd you get the job?"

"Remember I told you I got off the train

for a few minutes at Topeka to see an old friend?"

"Yeah."

"U.S. Marshal Jim Stokes. I worked for him as deputy marshal in St. Joe for several years. When he got the appointment as U.S. marshal, I became marshal of St. Joe. He's the one that lined me up with Barrigan."

Daley was about to explain his move in more detail when Curwood asked, "Georgetown pay a lot more?"

"Uh-huh," said Todd, blowing smoke through his nose. "Two hundred a month and fringe benefits."

"That *is* good," remarked Curwood. "So you don't know anyone in Georgetown?"

"Not a soul."

Unwittingly Todd Daley had just signed his own death warrant. The cold-blooded outlaw had it worked out in his mind. He would wait until after the train stopped in Abilene. He could keep Todd Daley awake with conversation. Once Abilene was behind them, he would lure the unsuspecting lawman out onto the platform. He must time it right so as to kill him just before the train reached the trestle eight miles west.

While over the trestle, Curwood would toss Daley's body into the river, minus his identification papers. The body would be a long way downstream before anybody would find it. Even when they did, it would be a good while before it would be identified. By that time, Dan Starr would be dead. Morey Barrigan would have given up a substantial amount of money . . . and Adam Curwood would be safely back in Lawrence.

Abilene had passed from sight and the train was back to top speed when the outlaw lit up a fresh cigar. He had kept Todd Daley awake with chatter, as planned. He looked at Daley and said, "Guess I'll step out to the platform at the rear of the car. Want to get some fresh air with me, Marshal?"

"Sure." Todd Daley smiled, standing up in the aisle.

Adam Curwood had not realized how tall Daley really was until he stood beside him. He figured the man must be at least six-feet-five, a half foot taller than Curwood. The two men stepped out on the platform and closed the door.

"Beautiful night, isn't it?" said Curwood, raising his voice above the roar of the moving train.

"Sure is," replied Daley, doing the same. While the taller man stared at the stars overhead the outlaw decided he would use the derringer, rather than the .45 on his hip. The .45 would be too loud. The sound of the smaller gun would be drowned out by the roar of the thundering wheels.

Curwood glanced into the car behind them, then looked over his shoulder through the window of the door through which he and Daley had just come. No one was stirring. Quickly he reached in his inside coat pocket and cocked the small weapon. The lawman was still concentrating on the heavens.

Curwood pulled out the derringer and raised the two vertically forged muzzles to the base of Daley's skull. The gun fired and the tall man jerked. Daley's hat flew off and whirled away into the darkness as his knees buckled. Curwood seized him by the collar and eased him down into a sitting position, making sure he did not go over the rail. Quickly he reached into the dead man's coat and produced his wallet. Making sure there was no other means of identification on the body, he jammed the wallet and the derringer into his own coat pocket.

Hurriedly the killer grasped the rail and moved down the metal steps. Narrowing his eyes against the wind, he peered up ahead. His timing had been perfect. He could see the dim outline of the trestle moving up fast.

Curwood climbed back to the platform and slid the inert form to the edge. In less than two minutes the train was over the trestle. With one giant heave, Todd Daley's body pitched over the narrow trestle and sailed downward like a rag doll. It plunged into the dark waters and was gone.

The early morning sun was bright against the mountaintops on the west side of Georgetown as seven riders wound around a crooked path on the opposite side of the valley and reined in. They sat their horses at the base of a giant, sheer rock wall. All around, gray-colored boulders stood like massive sentinels, overlooking the bustling town in the deep valley. Georgetown lay in the obscure shade of the towering peaks to the east.

A huge bald eagle left his perch on a craggy cliff and headed into the sun.

"Well, boys," said Tony Musio, "there it is. The town that is gonna make us rich."

"What're we sittin' here for?" asked Al Craig. "Let's get down there."

"Now hold on a minute," said the handsome, dark-complexioned Musio. "We've got to do this thing right. We can't all go riding in there at one time. Might arouse the citizens. I'll go in alone first. The town isn't too big, so I'll ride through slow. If Adam is there, he'll spot me. I'm going right to the mine office if he isn't there yet. I want to talk to that Sheffield dude. It'd be good if I got some answers from him before the boss arrives. After I've been there a half hour, Jim, you and Hutch ride down. I know you're hungry, so find an eating place and go on in."

Jim Hicks and Hutch Reiner nodded.

Looking at D.J. Salem and Al Craig, Musio said, "D.J., you and Al ride in twenty minutes later and find a place to eat. There may be only one café in town. If so, just act like you don't know Jim and Hutch."

"Gotcha," said Salem.

"If anybody gets nosy," said Musio, "tell them you're just passing through." Turning to the other two, he said, "You boys come in a half hour after D.J. and Al, okay? Get your bellies full, then mosey along the street. I'll slip up to you and tell you what's going on."

Nelson Blechman and Mike Poston nodded their assent. The seven unbathed, un-

135

shaven riders watched Tony Musio weave his horse down the mountainside and enter the town.

On his way down, the dark-eyed Musio studied the Barrigan mine, which was situated halfway up a copper-colored mountain to the southwest of Georgetown. Narrow-gauge ore carts, drawn by mules, were moving in and out of a large, dark aperture in the side of the mountain. The surrounding area was a beehive of activity. Tony's gaze was fixed on the piles of shiny earth in the carts. His desire for unlimited riches was exceeded only by his lust for beautiful women. With his looks he had experienced little trouble in satisfying the latter.

Musio reached the valley floor, then rode along the river until he reached the bridge on the east edge of town. Crossing the bridge, he rode slowly up the main street. On his right stood the marshal's office and jail. On his left he spotted the Alpine Café. He passed the hotel, the other business establishments, the saloon, and the Western Union office. Finally he turned off and rode to the mine office, which was at the base of the mountain where the mine loomed overhead.

There had been no sign of Adam Curwood.

Dismounting, Musio adjusted the black gun belt that held the two pearl-handled Colt .45s slung on his hips. He entered the office and encountered a young man who was just coming toward the door. The young man smiled and said, "Good morning. May I help you?"

"Yeah," said Musio. "I'm lookin' for a dude—er, I mean a gentleman named Derek Sheffield."

"You a friend of his?"

"Well, not exactly," replied Tony. "But he and I have a mutual friend. I was just passing through. Thought I'd stop and see him."

"Welcome to Georgetown," said the slender young man. "I'm Christopher John."

The black-haired man met Chris's grip. "Glad to meet you," he said, smiling weakly. "I'm Tony Musio."

"Just a minute, Mr. Musio," said Chris. "Derek's in the storeroom out back. I'll get him."

Just then a red-haired man came through the back door of the office. "Oh, here he is now," said Chris. "Derek, this gentleman

137

is here to see you." With that, Chris John moved out the door, leaving them alone.

Derek eyed the low-slung guns and the dark, granite face. His knees went weak.

"My name's Tony Musio," said the man without offering his hand. "You and I have a mutual friend. He asked me to drop in and see you."

"Oh, really?"

"Yeah. Adam Curwood."

Sheffield's face blanched.

"Seems there was a little mix-up on the train a few nights ago," said Musio, almost casually.

Sheffield cleared his throat. "I . . . I . . . I can explain the whole thing," he finally managed to say.

Musio slacked onto a straight-backed chair beside Sheffield's paper-strewn desk. Thumbing his hat to the back of his head, he said, "I'm all ears."

VII

As a timorous Derek Sheffield stuttered through his explanation of the change in dates on the payroll shipment, Jim Hicks and Hutch Reiner slid from their saddles and entered the Alpine Café. They had seen a tall, muscular man wearing a badge and a pair of twin Colts leave the café and cross the street to the marshal's office.

The Alpine was a busy place. The two outlaws saw a delicious-looking blonde in a cotton-print dress, cleaning off the only empty table. Hutch Reiner elbowed his partner and pointed with his chin. "Take a look at that, Jim," he said, threading among the tables. "I'm likin' Colorado better all the time."

Reiner was a big, stoop-shouldered man, just over six feet tall. Jo-Beth Taylor had her back to him as she ran a wet rag over the table. She straightened up, making a half turn, bumped into Reiner and stumbled. Quickly the ponderous man grasped her and pulled her close to him.

"You can let go now," said Jo-Beth, her voice losing its pleasantness.

Reiner guffawed and squeezed her tighter. Customers were now watching in disgust, and tension was mounting.

"I said let go," Jo-Beth hissed through clenched teeth.

Reiner laughed and released her. The tension eased. The little Chinaman had just started through the kitchen door, a meat cleaver in his hand. He checked himself when Jo-Beth was let go.

Reiner was still laughing as he sat down. Jim Hicks said to Jo-Beth, "Please don't mind him, ma'am. He don't mean no harm."

Jo-Beth straightened her crinkled dress and looked hard at Hicks. "You tell him to keep his paws to himself."

"Yes, ma'am," said Hicks. "Can we still get some breakfast?"

"I suppose," she snapped. "Breakfast is ham, eggs, fried potatoes, and coffee."

"That's fine, ma'am," said Hicks.

"Make mine a double portion," said Reiner, grinning wickedly. He pulled off his grimy hat and laid it on an empty chair.

Not bothering to reply, Jo-Beth turned toward the kitchen.

Jim Hicks and Hutch Reiner had just been served their meals when D.J. Salem and Al Craig came in. The table next to Hicks and Reiner was empty. The newcomers sat down, ignoring their partners in crime.

Jo-Beth took their order. Customers came and went. Reiner was just finishing his double portion when two more members of the gang, Blechman and Poston, moved through the door. They took a table across the room.

"C'mon, Hutch," said Jim Hicks in a low tone. "Hurry up. Tony don't want us all in one spot. We better get out on the street."

Reiner mumbled something indistinguishable and stuffed more food in his mouth. He chewed it briefly, swallowed, and washed it down with coffee. Jo-Beth walked by and he eyed her.

"Better leave her alone, Hutch," warned Hicks. "Tony don't want us bein' conspicuous. You're just askin' for trouble."

"Musio don't own me," growled the stoop-shouldered man.

Reiner was draining his coffee cup when Jo-Beth came by, moving from Craig and Salem's table. A pitcher of water was in her right hand. Reiner reached out, grabbed her empty hand, and pulled her toward him.

"Look, mister," said the young woman, "you've had your meal, now why don't you go on about your business?"

"I've decided to make *you* my business, baby," laughed the big man. "Here, come sit on Hutch's lap."

"Hutch . . ." warned Jim.

"Shut up, Hicks," snapped Reiner without looking at him.

Jo-Beth struggled against the man's powerful grip. "You're hurting me," she said

141

angrily. "Let go!" With that she poured the ice-cold water on his head.

Reiner gasped, then roared with laughter, pulling her down onto his lap. A customer waiting at the counter to pay his bill dashed out the door and headed across the street for the marshal's office.

The little Chinaman, hearing Jo-Beth's angry voice, came through the kitchen door with the meat cleaver. D.J. Salem, at the next table, saw him coming. Quickly Salem stood up, whipped out his pistol, and brought it down savagely on Tinky's head. The little cook slumped to the floor. Jo-Beth screamed and swung the empty glass pitcher at Reiner's head. The glass shattered, cutting the big man's face. He howled, letting go of her hand. Jo-Beth rushed toward Tinky, calling his name.

Suddenly Dave Bradford's silhouetted frame filled the door. "What's going on in here?" he bellowed. Customers froze in their chairs.

"These beasts hit Tinky in the head!" cried Jo-Beth from where she knelt on the floor.

Dave's eyes were fixed on Reiner and Salem. Speaking to Jo-Beth, he said, "Is he all right?"

"He's still breathing," she replied.

"What started it?" demanded Dave.

Jim Hicks eased out of his chair. Pointing a thumb at Reiner, he said, "My partner here was just funnin' a little bit with the waitress, Marshal. He didn't mean no harm. The Chinaman came at him with a meat cleaver." Turning the thumb toward Salem, he said, "This gentleman here had to whop him. He would've killed Hutch."

Dave's line of sight narrowed on Hutch Reiner's bleeding face. He was dabbing at it with a filthy bandanna. "How'd you get your face cut, mister?"

"I did it, Dan," said Jo-Beth from the floor. "Hit him with a water pitcher."

Dave scowled. Looking hard at Hicks, he said, "Just funnin', huh?" Swinging his gaze back to Reiner, he said, "You get on your horse and ride, mister. Don't let me see your ugly puss in this town again."

Reiner's hand started downward toward his gun. Jim Hicks grabbed his wrist. "Don't be a fool, Hutch!" he snapped. "That's Dan Starr you're lookin' at."

In the heat of anger Reiner had forgotten who was marshal of Georgetown. His features stiffened. "Let's get out of here, Jim," he said, reaching toward the empty chair for his hat.

Still blocking the door, Dave looked at two townsmen who sat at a table nearby. "You men take Tinky over to Doc Rice's office, will you?"

Instantly the pair went to the Chinaman, who was now conscious. They hoisted him up, each wrapping one of Tinky's arms around his neck. Blood ran in a steady stream down his temple. The two men moved outside and headed down the boardwalk with the injured cook.

Jo-Beth was standing where Tinky had fallen, rubbing her wrist and hand. Hutch Reiner had donned his hat, but was still dabbing at his bleeding face.

Dave nodded at her. "Jo-Beth, come here."

The woman threw Reiner a malignant look as she stepped around him and moved toward the marshal.

"Did he hurt you?" asked Dave.

"It's all right," she said, tossing hair from her eyes.

Dave took her hand between his fingers. There were marks on her wrist where Reiner's grip had borne down. He looked into Jo-Beth's wan face, shifted his gaze toward Reiner, and said softly, "Move aside, Jo-Beth. I reckon this fellow has a lesson coming to him."

While Dave Bradford was restoring order in the Alpine Café, Derek Sheffield had just finished explaining the change in the payroll shipping date, laying the blame for it on the tall, blond marshal. Tony Musio asked when it was coming.

"It will arrive in Denver tomorrow afternoon," Sheffield said. "Wells Fargo is responsible for getting it here from Denver. They vary the route and the timing of it. So it will be here either about dark tomorrow or sometime the next morning."

Musio's face went glum. "Be pretty tough to set up a robbery with a situation like that."

"That's the reason they do it that way."

Musio rubbed his chin and thought for a long moment. There was a strong possibility the payroll would be in Georgetown by nightfall tomorrow. It was up to him to figure out a plan.

"What are you thinking?" asked Sheffield.

Musio cocked his head sideways. "I'm thinking of a way to get my hands on that payroll and . . ."

"And what?"

"Derek, boy," said Musio, "if you'll help me work out a way to take a few sacks of gold nuggets along with the payroll, I'll see that you're cut in big on the gold too."

Sheffield's avaricious mind was quick to produce a solution. "I know how you can do it," he said with an eager look in his eyes.

"I'm listening."

"How many men do you have?"

"Seven, including me."

"That's plenty," said Sheffield.

"Well, come on, boy," said Musio excitedly, "let's hear it."

"If your gang would take over the Barrigan house with everybody in it except the old man, you'd have him by the nose."

"The nose?" Musio nodded, a smile spreading across his dark face. "Go on. I'm listening."

"Barrigan's house is built right into the mountains straight south of town. It's up about a quarter of a mile. There's a wagon trail leading to it. The thing is a virtual fort, ringed by a hundred feet of thick trees. Barrigan still has two kids at home. A daughter of twenty and a boy of sixteen.

You could hold his wife and those two kids hostage."

"You're makin' sense, man," said Musio.

Sheffield laughed. "The old boy would be forced to deliver the payroll right into your hands!"

Musio pursed his lips, his eyes gleaming. "Yeah . . . and all the gold we wanted too!"

"You're catching on." Sheffield chuckled. "I'll be right alongside Barrigan all the time. I'll prod him to do anything you say. After all, no amount of money can buy back the lives of his wife and kids."

Musio frowned. "Hey, come to think of it, seems to me Adam said Barrigan was your father-in-law."

Sheffield laughed coldly. "Yeah. That's right."

Shaking his head, the dark-haired outlaw said, "I can't figure you."

"Simple," said Sheffield. "He's getting filthy rich, and I'm stuck with a salary. I love my wife, but I couldn't care less what happens to the rest of the family. Especially when there's money in it for me. Big money!"

Musio hunched his shoulders, then let them drop. "I can guarantee you twenty-five percent of the gold too."

"Good enough." Sheffield smiled. "When you ride out, you simply take a couple of the family with you as hostages. That'll keep Barrigan off your back. You can turn them loose after you get far enough away."

"All right," agreed Musio. "Now, there's one other thing."

"What's that?"

"Your hotshot marshal, Dan Starr. He could give us trouble. They tell me he's tough, and fast as a whip."

"I could help you get him off guard," said Sheffield. "I hate his guts. Be glad to help you along that line."

"Good," said Musio. "You can help me find a way to get Starr up to the house after we take it over. We'll make him a hostage too. When we leave, we'll take him with us. My boss is after his hide. I'll just deliver Starr to him personally."

Sheffield grinned. He would be glad to be rid of Dan Starr.

"Say," said Musio, "as smart as you are for this kind of thing, you ought to chuck this job and throw in with us."

Sheffield shook his head. "Nope. I'll do just fine with my cut of the payroll and the gold. Running all over the country's not for me. My wife and kids are my whole life."

"How much gold can we get?" asked Musio.

"If you ride away with eight bags weighing twenty-five pounds apiece," said Morey Barrigan's treacherous son-in-law, "that would be over sixty thousand dollars' worth. Even after you left off my cut, you'd have plenty."

Musio agreed. Plans were quickly formed for subduing Dan Starr and taking over the Barrigan house. It would be done the next morning, when Morey had left the house. They would need him outside to carry through their demands.

The two men agreed on the place where the outlaws would leave Sheffield's part of the loot. Sheffield told Musio of his scheme to make Shirley think he had won the money gambling in Denver, then Musio left the office.

As the dark-eyed outlaw rode back and drew near the Alpine Café, he saw Hutch Reiner fly out of the door and land hard on his back. A tall man wearing a badge plunged after him.

Musio dismounted on the edge of the crowd that had gathered. Weaving through the onlookers, he watched the tall man pummel Reiner as Jim Hicks put in an appearance and threw a glance at him. A combination of punches laid Reiner out cold. The tall marshal eyed Jim Hicks and said, "Now you pick up that pile of pig meat and get out of town."

Hicks's eyes met Musio's. The latter gave him the sign to obey the marshal's order.

Musio waited until Hicks and the unconscious Reiner had disappeared at the east end of town, then entered the Alpine Café to fill his growling stomach.

Tony Musio gathered the Curwood gang a mile east of town in late afternoon. They dismounted in a narrow canyon lined with fluttering aspens and divided by a rushing river.

While the shadows lengthened Musio laid out the plan, which would go into action at sunup the next morning. Since there was only one way up to the Barrigan house, the gang would wait among the trees north of the main street at the west end of town. As soon as Morey Barrigan descended the steep trail and entered his office at the mine, they would spur their horses upward and close in on the house.

Once the house and hostages were secured, D.J. Salem would go down and hit

Barrigan with the bad news, presenting their demands. The mineowner would have no choice but to meet them. The lives of Dottie, Emily, and Brett Barrigan would be at stake. And if everything worked as planned, Dan Starr would also become a hostage.

Satisfied their plan was foolproof, the gang separated and filtered back into town, minus Hutch Reiner and Jim Hicks, who set up camp beside the river and would join the others later.

Dave Bradford sat at a table in the Alpine Café, picking carelessly at his supper, his insides knotted. He had fallen hopelessly in love with the beautiful Jo-Beth, and he could no longer deceive her. He told himself he should never have allowed their friendship to develop this far. The truth was going to have to come out soon, and he must pick the right time and place to tell her.

It would have been easier if Jo-Beth had not fallen in love with him—but in actuality, he thought, it was not him. She was in love with Dan Starr. She was going to be hurt when she learned he had been deceiving her, that he was actually a hunted outlaw. Deeply hurt.

When Dave was leaving the café, Nelson Blechman and Mike Poston approached the door on the boardwalk. "Evening, gentle-men," he said, nodding.

"Evenin', Marshal," the outlaws said in chorus.

As the two men moved in and sat down at a table, Poston said in a subdued voice, "I hate to see what's going to happen to that lawman when we tie him up in Barrigan's house. Hutch will probably beat him to death."

"He might bruise him up a little bit," said Blechman, "but Tony won't let Hutch kill him. He's saving him for the boss, re-member?"

"You're right," agreed Poston. "But ol' Hutch will cripple him for sure!"

At closing time Jo-Beth and Tinky stepped out of the café. Dave had already made his rounds and was waiting on the boardwalk. Tinky's head was bandaged, but he was feeling better.

"Good night, Miss Taylor," said the little man, bowing.

"Good night, Tinky." Jo-Beth planted a kiss on the cook's cheek. "Thank you for what you did for me this morning."

"All Tinky do is get hit on head, but I am velly glad Miss Taylor not get hurt."

The serious little man actually appeared to be blushing.

Dave said good night to Tinky, who bowed in return, then was gone.

Jo-Beth smiled and took Dave's arm. As they strolled toward her house she said, from out of the blue, "Dan, do you want to talk about it?"

Dave felt his tongue go numb. "What . . . uh . . . what's that?"

"I love you, darling. I can tell something is bothering you. It isn't like you to leave food on your plate. Are you having second thoughts about leaving Georgetown?"

Dave squeezed her hand where it gripped his arm. "I . . ." He swallowed hard.

"You *are* considering staying, aren't you?" she said, stopping and looking at him excitedly. Wrapping her arms around his neck, she pulled him down and kissed him warmly.

Dave cursed his own weakness. This lovely young woman totally destroyed his resolution. He was helplessly in love with her. It was going to break his heart to leave her—but leave her he must.

Tomorrow, he told himself. *In the daytime. I'll talk to her at the marshal's office. Nothing romantic about that place. Yes, that's it. To-morrow. At the office.*

VIII

Seven determined men sat their horses within the trees near the western end of Georgetown's main street. The gray of dawn transformed to a golden sunrise while they watched the steep wagon ruts leading up to the Barrigan house.

The mine workers were on the job at first light. As they filed down the street, crossed the bridge, and climbed to the mine, the Curwood gang watched with interest.

"Go ahead, boys," said D.J. Salem in a low voice. "Dig it out for us. We're goin' to take a load of your gold when we go."

"Yeah," chimed in Nelson Blechman. "We're going to be rich!"

While the outlaws waited for Morey Barrigan to put in an appearance, Derek Sheffield was preparing to leave for work. The Sheffield house was two blocks off the main street, just north of the Georgetown Bank, in the center of town.

Sheffield took Shirley in his arms and

kissed her. "Sure am glad you're home, honey," he said tenderly. "I missed you while you were away."

Shirley cuddled close to him, coyly rubbing the tip of his chin with her forefinger. "Did you really miss me?"

"You know I did," he said.

"Oh, I bet you wouldn't care if I never came back," teased Shirley.

Firming his hold on her, he said seriously, "Don't even talk that way, Shirley. If I ever lost you, I'd go out of my mind."

"You mean it?" she said, still toying with his chin.

"You're my whole life, darling. I wouldn't even want to live without you."

They kissed long and tenderly. As Sheffield started toward the door he asked, "What are you going to do today?"

"You mean other than feed the kids when they wake up . . . and wash clothes . . . and be a mother . . . and everything else a woman does?"

"Yeah."

"Well, I'm going to begin making myself a new dress today."

Sheffield paused with his hand on the doorknob. "If we had more money, you wouldn't have to make your dresses."

"Derek, you worry too much about the money we don't have. We have enough. Daddy pays you well. Besides, I enjoy making my clothes. Mother still makes a lot of her own clothes. We both find it fun and relaxing."

"Okay." He smiled. "Every man to his own poison." He paused, then said, "Honey, you wouldn't mind if on my next trip to Denver I gambled a few dollars, would you?"

Shirley gave him a sober look. "What do you mean?"

"Well," said Sheffield, "The last time I was there, I saw this man playing some new card game at the casino in the Brown Palace Hotel. He was winning money hand over fist. Said he'd let me in on his secret if I'd play my own game and give him a small cut on my winnings."

"I don't mind, honey," responded Shirley, "as long as you set yourself a limit on how much you'll lost and quit when you hit the limit."

"Can't lost on this one, sweet stuff." Sheffield chuckled. Blowing her a kiss, he stepped out into the brisk morning air. He was pleased with himself. He had broken the ice on his plan for coming up with sudden riches.

Shirley Sheffield tiptoed into the room where her children slept. Since they were still sleeping soundly, she decided to go ahead and begin her new dress. She laid her sewing basket on the dining room table and spread out the necessary items. It was then that she discovered her pattern was missing. She remembered that she had lent it to her sister Emily before the Kansas City trip.

Moving to the rear of the house, Shirley went out the back door and crossed the yard. Georgetown was still in the shade of the ragged peaks to the east, but the rising sun was shooting fan-shaped streamers over the mountains into the crystal sky. Shirley stepped up on the back porch of the neighbor's house straight behind her own and rapped on the door.

Presently the door swung open, revealing a fortyish woman with her hair in a kerchief. "Good morning, Shirley," she said cheerfully. "Come for some coffee?"

"Not this time, Erline," replied Shirley. "I was wondering if Rhonda is up."

"Sure is," said Erline Thomas.

"Could she come over and stay with Timmy and the baby for a while? I need to run up to my mother's and pick up a pattern. Going to start on a new dress today. The children are still asleep."

"Certainly," said Erline. Turning, she called, "Rhonda!"

Tony Musio and his cohorts watched Christopher and Merilee John come down the street together and cross the bridge. Just across the bridge, they parted. Chris moved toward the mine office, and his slender wife began the climb to Barrigan's house. The mineowner had not shown up yet.

"Looks like we'll have us another hostage, Tony," piped up Al Craig.

"The more we have, the greater our bargaining power," said Musio.

Hutch Reiner, who dwarfed the horse he sat on, looked at the dark, handsome man and said, "Tony, what we gonna do if Barrigan ain't bargaining?"

Musio was pulling a cigarillo from his shirt pocket. He produced a match and thumbed it into flame. Cupping his hands around the cigarillo tip against the morning breeze, he looked at the stoop-shouldered man and said coldly, "We'll start killing hostages until Old Moneybags comes through."

Jim Hicks laughed. "Well, I guess one or two corpses will loosen his purse strings."

Musio spoke up and said, "Hey, boys. There goes Judas Iscariot."

All eyes focused on Derek Sheffield as he moved down the street at a fast walk, crossed the bridge, and entered the mine office.

"Yeah," chuckled D.J. Salem. "And he ain't even goin' to get his thirty pieces of silver!"

The whole bunch had a good laugh.

Fifteen minutes passed.

"Hey, Tony," said Hutch Reiner, "lookee there."

Hutch was pointing at a pretty young woman who came from the street and moved across the bridge. She walked briskly and headed up the steep incline.

Suddenly, from the dense trees higher up, they saw a square-shouldered man emerge.

Pointing, D.J. Salem said, "Tony, that's gotta be Barrigan."

"That's him all right," said Musio, blowing smoke.

From their vantage point the gang watched Morey Barrigan stop halfway down the steep slope and talk to his oldest daughter. The conversation was short. Barrigan headed on down. Shirley moved upward.

"Well," said Craig, "add one more to the hostage list. Wonder who those two women are?"

"Who cares?" clipped Blechman. "Like Tony says, more bargaining power."

"Get ready, boys," said Musio. "As soon as Old Moneybags pops into the office, we go."

Three minutes' time put Morey Barrigan into the mine office.

Tony Musio kicked his horse's sides and thundered up the steep double-rutted path. The others were quickly on his heels. The horses slowed as they reached the thick stand of trees. There was no one in sight when the outlaws reined in at the front of the house. A big black and white shaggy dog sprang off the porch, barking ferociously.

Merilee John was cleaning in a front bedroom upstairs when she heard the drumming of the hooves, followed by Mutt's wild barking. Looking out the window, she saw the seven men dismounting. One of them picked up a rock and threw it at Mutt. The dog yelped and dived under the porch. Quickly Merilee wheeled and darted from the room. Reaching the top of the stairs, she yelled, "Mrs. Barrigan! Lock the door! Hurry!"

Dottie Barrigan came from the rear of the house on the main floor, her two daughters following. She threw a glance at Merilee, who was plunging down the stairs. At the same instant the door burst open.

Tony Musio appeared, both guns drawn. "Everybody hold it right there!" he barked.

Dottie's face lost its color. The room was suddenly full of bearded, unbathed men. Emily, Shirley, and Merilee gathered close to the older woman. "What do you want?" demanded Dottie, eyes wide.

Abruptly Brett Barrigan came out of his upstairs room and looked down at the scene from the top of the stairs. He turned to dart back into his room. Musio bellowed, "Hold it right there, kid!"

Brett paused, then ran for his room. Both of Tony's guns roared, the bullets chewing the door frame just in front of the youth.

Merilee screamed.

Brett stopped instantly. As he slowly turned around, Musio looked through the blue smoke that hung like fog in the room and said, "Make another move like that, kid, and I'll blow your head off. Now you come down here!"

Pale and weak-kneed, Brett descended the stairs.

"What do you want?" asked Dottie tremulously.

"Not much, Mrs. Moneybags," sneered Musio. "Just the mine payroll and a few sacks of gold. Your husband will provide all of it, once he learns that we've got his family up here." Swinging his gaze to Merilee, he snapped, "Who are you?"

"I—I'm the maid," said Merilee.

"What's your name?"

"M-Merilee John."

Then Musio turned to Shirley. "And who are you, baby?"

Shirley's face flushed. "I'm Shirley Sheffield."

"Oh." The dark man grinned viciously. "You're the oldest daughter here. You're the one that's married to Mr. Iscariot."

Shirley looked confused. Shaking her head, she said, "No, my husband's name is Derek Sheffield."

"Yeah," chuckled Musio. "Judas Iscariot."

Still confused, Shirley bit her lip and looked searchingly at her mother.

"All right, everybody," said Tony Musio with a note of authority, "we're going to be roommates for a little while. I want you all in the parlor here. No one leaves the room unless I say so."

While the outlaws herded the five frightened people to sitting places, Musio holstered his guns and spoke to D.J. Salem. "Okay, D.J., go break the news to Barrigan and tell him we know that the payroll is to be here today. He'd better produce it. The two hundred pounds of gold too. Get Sheffield on his mission."

Shirley Sheffield eyed Musio quizzically.

D.J. Salem left, slamming the door behind him.

Derek Sheffield looked up from his desk as D.J. Salem came through the office door. Across the room Christopher John also looked up. Salem winked at Sheffield and said, "I want to see Barrigan."

"*Mister* Barrigan is busy," said Sheffield, with a tone of loyalty to his employer.

Throwing a hard look at John, Salem said, "You, junior. Go tell your big boss I got somethin' real important to discuss with him."

The tone of the man's voice brought Chris out of his chair. "I'll get him," he said, heading for a rear office.

At the same moment Derek Sheffield,

nodding to Salem, plunged out the door, heading for the marshal's office.

Dave Bradford sat in the office, still upset. A sleepless night had left his eyes dull and bloodshot, and at breakfast he had asked Jo-Beth to come and talk to him as soon as the customers thinned out.

The beautiful woman was now coming across the dusty street. Dave's heart thundered in his chest. He was about to do the hardest thing he had ever done.

Jo-Beth came through the door, smiling.

Oh, you're so beautiful, Dave said to himself. *Why do things have to be like this?*

Jo-Beth moved toward him and slid her arms around his neck. "You're going to stay, aren't you, darling?" she said. "I just know what you're going to tell me."

"Jo-Beth," said Dave, unable to meet her gaze, "I'm not . . . I'm not who you think I am."

The woman tilted her head and blinked. "I don't understand, darling."

Suddenly, heavy rapid footsteps sounded on the boardwalk outside and Derek Sheffield burst inside. Breathlessly, he gasped, "Marshal! We got trouble at the mine office! You've got to come right now!"

164

Dave looked past Jo-Beth and asked, "What is it, Derek?"

"I'll explain on the way. Quick!"

Turning to Jo-Beth, Dave said, "Honey, I'll talk to you later."

"Certainly, darling," she replied. "You go and take care of the trouble. Be careful."

Jo-Beth watched the two men charge westward while she slowly crossed the street.

Running alongside Sheffield, Dave said, "What's going on?"

"A rough-looking man came into the office demanding to see Mr. Barrigan. He sounded threatening."

Dave asked no more. He would find out what it was about in a few seconds.

As they approached the mine office Sheffield drew back, saying, "I'll wait out here."

Dave nodded, loosened his guns in their holsters, and moved inside. D.J. Salem was sitting behind Chris John's desk with a smug look on his face. Morey Barrigan was bent over in a chair in the middle of the room, his shoulders drooped. His face was as white as death. Chris John stood beside him, his own features drawn and grim.

"Come in, Marshal Starr," Salem said in a cold, steady voice. "We've been waitin' for you."

"What's going on?" demanded Dave, closing the door.

Barrigan looked at the tall man. There was fear in his eyes. "Gang of outlaws have taken over my house," he said, choking on the words. "They've got Dottie and the kids. Shirley and Merilee are up there too."

Dave glared at D.J. Salem. "And you're the spokesman, huh?"

"Yep." Salem nodded. His smile was caustic.

"What do you want?"

"Nothin' but the little ol' payroll when it arrives today. That, and a couple hundred pounds of gold."

"How many men you have up there?" asked Dave.

Salem stood up, shoving the chair back. "You'll find out when we get there."

"*We?*"

"Yeah, lawman. You and me. We don't want you running around loose, getting into trouble. Take off your guns."

After a moment's hesitation Dave begun untying the thongs on his muscular thighs.

Chris John spoke up quickly, "Mr. Starr! Don't take your guns off! Don't—"

"Have to, Chris," said Dave. "I know what this bird is going to say next. His buddies up there at the house are expecting him back by a certain time. If he doesn't show up by then, they start killing hostages."

Chris's face stiffened.

"Hey, lawman," said Salem with a throaty chuckle, "you're pretty smart. You should have been an outlaw, 'stead of pinnin' on that stupid badge."

If only you knew, Dave thought.

"What are we going to do?" asked the wan-faced mineowner.

"Well, at this point," replied Dave, "I'd say you'd better start stacking gold and make plans to deliver them the payroll money as soon as it arrives."

"Now that's right smart advice, Marshal," said Salem, grinning wickedly.

Barrigan swore, wiping cold sweat from his forehead. Dave laid his holster and guns on Derek Sheffield's desk. "I'll take those," said Salem, picking up the heavy double-holstered belt and slinging it over his shoulder. "Let's go, Starr."

Chris John took a step toward Salem. "You'd better not hurt my wife, mister," he said, his tone both fearful and angry.

Salem, who had not bothered to draw

his gun, eyed him blandly. "If your boss here cooperates, nobody'll get hurt."

"Don't worry, Chris," Barrigan spoke up. "I'll see they get what they want. No amount of money in the world is worth getting those we love hurt."

"That's good clear thinkin'," said Salem. "Now I'm goin' to repeat what I told you before the marshal showed up. I want you to bring up the payroll and two hundred pounds of gold, personally. When you reach the edge of the trees in front of your house, you sing out for Tony Musio. We'll watch you lay the payroll and the sacks of gold on the ground in plain sight. Got it?"

"I've got it," said Barrigan, nodding.

"We've got men with rifles stationed at the windows," continued Salem. "If anybody but you sticks his face around them trees, he'll get it blowed off and we'll turn your parlor into a slaughterhouse. You got it?"

Barrigan nodded solemnly.

"And another thing," said the outlaw. "When we ride outta this burg, if anybody tries to stop us or trail us with a posse, we'll kill your beloved marshal. He's goin' with us. At least one of the females will be goin' along too. So if you want to see bloodshed, you just try trailin' us with a posse. Have I made myself clear, Barrigan?"

"You have," answered the mineowner, shaking his head and looking at the floor.

"All right, Marshal," said Salem, tossing his head toward the door, "let's go climb the mountain."

Dave opened the door. Salem looked at the mineowner and said, "We'll be listenin' for your voice before sundown, Barrigan. You'd better pray that payroll gets here from Denver by then."

As Dave and the determined outlaw stepped out of the office, Clarence Sheets was coming toward them at a brisk walk.

Salem spoke in a low voice. "If this little guy acts like he notices I'm carryin' your guns, he'll have to climb the mountain with us."

Dave did not reply. He was looking around for Derek Sheffield, who was nowhere in sight. Now there was no doubt in his mind—Sheffield was an accomplice of the outlaws. *These must be the same men who held up the train in Kansas*, he thought.

The little telegraph operator paid no attention to the two men leaving the mine office. Salem looked back and watched him pass through the door.

As they climbed the steep path Dave analyzed the situation. The outlaws totally had the advantage. The Barrigan house was a virtual fortress, with only one access to the place. The south side of the property had a small barn and corral where the horses and wagon were kept, and the back side of the barn rose from the edge of a sheer cliff. The cliff came around the east side, circular fashion, where it joined abruptly to the tree-lined slope on the north. The house was wedged into the mountain on the west. Coming from that direction, a man would have to walk on the roof. There would be no way to take the outlaws by surprise.

Morey Barrigan saw no alternative to turning over the payroll money to the outlaws as soon as it arrived. In the meantime two hundred pounds of gold nuggest had to be sacked and made ready.

Speaking to his bookkeeper, the mine-owner said, "Chris, find Derek and bring him in here."

At that instant Clarence Sheets came through the office door, a slip of paper in his hand. "Wire for you, Mr. Barrigan."

Barrigan took the message from Sheets, began reading, and swore as Chris John looked through a dusty window and said, "Here comes Derek now."

The mineowner finished reading the message, crumpled it up angrily, and swore again. Derek Sheffield entered, threw a quick glance at Clarence Sheets, then said, "What's the matter, Dad?"

"Plenty!" snapped Barrigan. Fixing a stiff glare on his son-in-law, he said, "Where'd you go after you went after the marshal?"

"I, uh . . . just moved back out in the trees," he replied nervously. "I figured as mean as the hombre looked, there might be some shooting, and one of us should be outside to get help, if needed." Feigning innocence, he said, "I saw him and the marshal head up toward your house. What's going on?"

"Gang of hoodlums has taken over the house," said Barrigan grimly. "They want the payroll money and two hundred pounds of gold."

Derek feigned a look of shock. "You mean they're holding Mom and the kids as hostages?"

While Barrigan nodded morosely Chris John spoke up. "And they've got Merilee too."

"Oh, no," said Derek, shaking his head.

"That's not all," added Barrigan. "They've got Shirley."

These last words hit Derek Sheffield like a sledgehammer. This time the shocked look on his face was not faked. Mouth agape, he stammered, "Sh-Shirley?"

"Yep."

"H-how did they g-get Shirley up there?"

Barrigan ran shaky fingers through his silver hair. "She went up to get a dress pattern that she'd lent to Emily. I met her while I was coming down to the office."

Sheffield went cold inside. Shirley was in the hands of those desperate men. Sweat beaded his brow. Quickly he tried to comfort himself with the thought that they wouldn't dare touch his wife. After all, he was the one who had set up this whole operation.

"But we've got more problems," said Barrigan glumly, interrupting Sheffield's thoughts. He held up the wad of paper. "Wire from the bank in Kansas City. Flood on the Solomon River in Kansas weakened a trestle. They've got to repair it before the trains can cross. Payroll money's going to be three or four days late."

"Well, all we can do is go up there and

172

tell those men about the delay," said Sheffield.

"I doubt they'll listen," groaned Barrigan. "They're liable to kill somebody."

Sheffield felt panic gripping him. He had not counted on Shirley's being one of the hostages. What if nobody up in the house bothered to tell Tony Musio who she was? Shirley had a lot of spunk. She just might try resisting Musio and his gang.

His voice unsteady, he said, "Morey, let's wire Kansas City and tell them to send the money all the way by stagecoach. That would shorten the time by a day."

"No," said Barrigan. "Somehow these criminals have been getting inside information about the payroll shipment. If the stage was robbed, we wouldn't have the money at all."

A flush of guilt surged through Sheffield.

"I'm afraid they'll never leave without the payroll," went on Barrigan. "The only thing I can do is go up there and talk to them. Explain about the trestle."

"Let me go with you," said Sheffield, knowing full well of Musio's plan to deal solely with Barrigan. But volunteering would make him look good.

"No," said the mineowner. "They'll only

talk with me. They made that very clear. The man that came in here said they'd shoot anybody else who stuck his face past the trees."

Clarence Sheets spoke up. "You want I should answer the wire, Mr. Barrigan?"

"Oh, uh, yes," replied the mineowner. "Tell them to put the money on the first train through. Double the guards . . . and wire us so we'll know when to expect it."

"Will do," replied the elderly man.

As Sheets disappeared through the door Barrigan said, "Derek, you go get the men started sacking gold. I doubt if we can get two hundred pounds by nightfall. Depends on what they've garnered since the last shipment." Turning to where Chris John had been standing, he said, "Chris, you—"

Barrigan's eyes searched the room. Chris was gone.

IX

Dave Bradford and D.J. Salem moved through the trees in the dappled sunlight. As they reached the timber's edge Salem motioned for Dave to stop. He removed his hat and waved it from behind a tall spruce. "Hey! Tony! It's me—D.J.! I got the marshal!"

"Come on in, D.J.!" came a deep-voiced reply.

Salem eyed Bradford. "Okay, Starr," he said, nodding toward the house. "Let's go."

As the two men approached, Mutt darted from under the porch and headed for Dave. Bounding to the tall man, the dog jumped at him in a friendly manner and licked Dave's hands, dancing along on his hind legs.

Dave slowed his pace, giving the shaggy animal his attention. "Hello, boy," he said, ruffling the fur on his neck.

"Forget the hound," rasped D.J. "Just get into the house."

"It's not going to hurt if I give the dog a little attention," Dave said in a crusty tone.

Salem took a step toward the hopping dog and kicked him savagely in the side, hollering, "Get out of here, you ugly hound!"

Mutt yelped, rolling in the dirt from the impact of the blow. Dave reacted instinctively, lashing out with a fist, which connected squarely with Salem's jaw. The outlaw went down in a crumpled heap.

175

"Hey!" came an exclamation from the house.

Four men suddenly thundered out the door, guns leveled. Dave was kneeling beside Mutt, helping the dazed animal get his breath. Mike Poston dropped down beside the unconscious Salem.

Craig, Blechman, and Reiner circled around Bradford. Cocking the hammer of his revolver, Al Craig snapped, "Get up, Starr! Leave the dog be."

Craig took two steps sideways, aimed the muzzle of his gun at Mutt's head, and squeezed the trigger. Dave jerked at the roar and watched the dog die instantly.

Fury shot through him like the bullet that had just shot through the air. A wild, savage cry escaped his lips. Craig started to thumb back the hammer again, but before he could Dave tackled him head-on. The savage impact knocked the outlaw's revolver from his hand, and the two men rolled on the ground. Hutch Reiner cocked his gun and was trying to draw a bead on Dave.

Tony Musio was suddenly at Reiner's side, touching his arm. "No, Hutch!" he warned. "Adam wants him."

Craig and Dave were now on their feet, fists flying.

Inside the house Jim Hicks was waving a gun at his captives, who were gathered at the parlor window. "Sit down, all of you!" bellowed Hicks.

"He killed our dog!" shouted Brett.

"I said sit down!" the outlaw bellowed. Slowly the youth and the four women obeyed.

Outside, Craig threw a wild punch and Dave sidestepped, saying angrily, "You had no call to kill that dog!" With that he slammed a left into the center of the man's face, and blood spurted from Craig's nose. He immediately followed with a rocking right, cracking Craig flush on the jaw. The outlaw flopped to his back, eyes glazed.

Tony Musio had just told Hutch Reiner to move in and hit the lawman on the head with his gun barrel. As Dave was regaining his balance the big man came up behind him. Dave made a half turn and saw the gun coming in a full arc. In the split second before the impact, he twisted. The hard steel caught him on the left cheek. His eyes blinked shut as he tasted warm blood, and he staggered like a drunken man.

Reiner's gun came down again, connecting on his skull. The whole world went into a spin. His head seemed to come loose from his neck. His body felt as if it were floating down into a pitch-black chasm . . .

There was a noisome buzzing in his head as it seemed to attach itself to his neck once more. His body floated upward out of the dark pit.

At first Dave thought he was paralyzed. His arms would not move. Neither would his legs. Voices soon overcame the volume of the roar inside his head. With effort he opened his eyes and blinked against the light. He focused on Emily Barrigan, who was weeping over the body of Mutt, which lay on the floor, just inside the door.

Then he realized he was lying on the parlor floor, bound hand and foot with lasso rope. His head throbbed with pain. There was a brassy taste in his mouth.

"Well," came the voice of Tony Musio, "our big marshal is back with us again. Dan Starr, the dog lover."

Dave eyed Musio malevolently as the dark-haired outlaw stood over him.

Hutch Reiner came into view. Looking down at the lawman with hungry eyes, he said, "How about me puttin' him back to sleep, Tony? I owe him for what he did to me at the café."

"We owe him too," said Salem. "Maybe we ought to take turns rearranging his face."

"Big, tough men, aren't you?" came Shirley Sheffield's challenge. She stood up from the sofa, where she had been seated beside her mother.

"You sit down, lady," rasped Musio, his hands resting on the butts of his pearl-handled .45s.

"Or you'll knock me down, right?" retaliated Shirley. "Big rugged men. There's not a one of you here that could handle Dan Starr in a fair fight. But you're rough stuff, aren't you? Not afraid to talk big while he's tied up."

Al Craig, his nose swollen and red, said curtly, "Tony told you to sit down, Mrs. Sheffield. Now you do it, or else."

"Or else what?" asked Shirley, a defiant look on her face. "You going to shoot me, like you shot the defenseless dog?"

Craig clenched his teeth. "Lady—"

Turning her attention to the outlaw leader, the impudent woman continued, "The least you could've done was leave Mutt's body outside. Why did you have to bring it in here?"

Tony Musio crossed the room, his face rigid. He looked dangerous, totally unpredictable. He said quietly, "The dog's corpse is in here to show you and the rest of this bunch how you'll end up if you give us trouble. Now sit down and be quiet."

He turned and walked away.

Shirley stayed on her feet, glaring heatedly at his back. Al Craig saw it and moved toward her swiftly. With open palm he slapped her hard, knocking her down on the sofa.

Brett Barrigan, who was seated in a straight-backed chair across the room, sprang from his position in a rage. He slammed into Craig with his shoulder. The impetus drove the two of them into a side window. The glass shattered, cutting Al's face and young Barrigan's hands.

Hutch Reiner dashed to them and seized Brett. He picked him up and threw him across the room. The youth landed on the floor and crashed into a china closet. Dishes rattled, some falling to the floor and shattering.

"Now look!" roared Reiner. "The next person who gets rambunctious dies! Everyone understand?"

Dottie Barrigan attended to her eldest

180

daughter, casting quick glances at Brett, who was picking himself off the floor.

Shirley adjusted herself on the sofa. Rubbing her beet-red cheek, she said to Reiner, "What did you expect, big man? My brother only did the natural thing. He would protect his sister. He's more of a man than any of you!"

"You shut your mouth, sister," clipped D.J. Salem. "If it weren't for your husband, none of you would be in this pickle."

"What's Derek got to do with this?" she countered angrily. When no one answered, she turned to Musio. "You called my husband Judas Iscariot. Why?"

The outlaws looked at one another furtively and laughed. "Shall I spill the beans, boys?" asked Musio.

"Go ahead, Tony," chortled Salem. "Sheffield ain't gettin' no cut anyway."

Musio strode to where Shirley sat on the sofa. Looking down with a smirk, he said, "Your husband's a Judas, ma'am. A traitor."

Shirley's features stiffened. "What do you mean?"

"He sold out your pa's big payroll, expecting to get a cut for himself."

Shirley's face reddened. "You're a dirty liar!"

"Am I?" asked Musio. "How do you think we knew about the payroll in the first place?"

"Well, you could have . . ."

"Could have what? How many people know just when the money's being shipped, Mrs. Sheffield?"

"My father sets the date," replied Shirley. "My husband sends the wire. So there are three people in Georgetown who know. Clarence Sheets taps out the message. Maybe it's Clarence. He could have contacted you."

"He could have, ma'am," said Musio, "but he didn't."

"Derek wouldn't steal from my father!" snapped Shirley.

"Seems like you don't know your husband very well, Mrs. Sheffield. It was his idea for us to come up here and hold your mother and these kids hostage. He thinks he's getting twenty-five percent of the payroll and the same cut of the gold we're taking out of here."

"Shut up!" said Shirley. "I won't listen to your lies! How would Derek come into that kind of money and not arouse suspicion? Especially from me?"

Musio smiled. "Simple," he said. "He told me he was going to tell you he won it gambling. He's planning to take his share of the gold to Denver and convert it to cash."

A nagging doubt was rising in Shirley's mind. Something her husband had said just this morning . . .

Musio's next statement made it all sickeningly clear. "He told me, ma'am, that he was going to give you some cock-and-bull story about a new card game at the Brown Palace Hotel in Denver."

Shirley Sheffield sunk low on the sofa.

Dottie looked at her and said, "Just don't you listen to that kind of talk, honey. He's making all of this up. Derek wouldn't—"

"It's true, Mother," Shirley cut in. "What he just said is true. Derek told me about this new card game he was going to play at the Brown Palace Hotel in Denver, said some gambler was going to show him how he could play it and get rich. He couldn't miss." Shirley's face grayed and pinched. "Oh, Mother, it's true. Derek is working with these outlaws. He *is* a Judas!"

Dottie Barrigan was at a loss for words.

Brett spoke up from near the broken window. "Mom, could you help me? Both my hands are bleeding."

Dottie looked up at Musio. "Go ahead," said the dark-eyed outlaw.

Al Craig was dabbing at his bleeding face with a bandanna. Dottie stood up and headed toward the staircase.

"Where you goin'?" demanded Hutch Reiner.

Pausing, Dottie said, "Upstairs. I need to get bandages and iodine to put on their cuts." Swinging her eyes to Craig, she said, "I'll tend to you too. Even if you are a dog killer."

"You go up with her, Hutch," said Musio. "Watch her."

Just as Dottie and Reiner disappeared up the stairs Jim Hicks hollered at Musio, "Hey, Tony! Some guy's movin' around out there in the trees!"

Musio dashed to where Hicks and Mike Poston sat, watching through a large window.

"It better be Barrigan," he said, peering toward the dense timber.

D.J. Salem was immediately beside Musio. "I made it clear to him, Tony. I told him if anybody but him stuck his face out of those trees, we'd blow it off."

Suddenly a slender figure appeared in the shade of the tall timber. His voice cut the morning air. "Merilee! Merilee! Are you all right?"

Merilee John jumped up from where she sat. "It's Chris!" she gasped. She ran to the door and flung it open. Nelson Belchman grasped her just as she shouted, "Chris! Go back! They'll shoot you!"

"Merilee!" came Chris's voice. "Tell them I want to talk to their leader!"

"Get her away from the door, Nelson," said Musio. As Blechman obeyed, dragging Merilee back, Musio moved near the door without exposing himself. Lifting his voice, he said, "We're dealing with nobody but Barrigan! Now you get out of here, or we'll kill your wife!"

"Please, mister," Chris called from the shadows, "I've come to offer myself as a hostage in place of my wife. I'm unarmed. Will you let her go if I come in?"

"Don't do it, Chris!" shouted Merilee. "They'll kill you!"

"Shut her up, Nelson," commanded Musio.

Nelson Blechman swung a punch that slammed against Merilee's jaw. She went down hard, unconscious. Dave struggled furiously against the ropes that held him tight, his eyes wild. Brett Barrigan, his hands still bleeding, started for Blechman. D.J. Salem whipped out his revolver and dogged back the hammer. Brett checked himself.

"Back to where you were, kid," Salem said icily.

His hatred clear on his face, Brett moved slowly back to his place, looking down at Dave Bradford.

Dottie Barrigan came down the stairs, her hands loaded, with Reiner on her heels. "What's going on?" she asked, eyeing the inert form of Merilee John on the floor.

"It's Chris, Mother," spoke up Shirley. "He's offering to trade himself for Merilee as a hostage. She just called for Chris not to try it."

Dottie shook her head, glared at Blechman, then turned her attention to Brett and Al Craig.

"What about it?" came Chris John's call.

"Sure!" hollered Tony Musio. "Come on in!"

Dave knew exactly what was going to happen. These men were anxious to apply as much leverage as possible on Morey Barrigan. A dead bookkeeper who had gone against their orders would put a sharp spur in Barrigan's side.

Outside, Chris John moved toward the

sunlight. "Let her come out on the porch," he called. "I want to see her."

"You just come in here first!" bellowed a voice from the dark interior. "Then we'll turn her loose!"

Desperate for Merilee's safety, Chris stepped out into the bright sunlight, empty hands held high. At the same instant Dave Bradford's voice came from inside the house, "Don't do it, Chris! Get back!"

But it was too late. Tony Musio's right-hand .45 roared. Chris felt the impact of the bullet as it slammed his left shoulder. Only the thirty-yard distance kept it from accurately hitting his heart. A second bullet bit the dirt next to him as the wounded book-keeper crawled toward the safety of the trees. A third split bark from a cedar and whined away as Chris wriggled into the shadows.

Inside the house Hutch Reiner kicked Dave Bradford in the head.

Chris struggled, trying to get on his feet. As he did, he saw Morey Barrigan climbing down the steep slope toward him at a fast pace. Chris gained his feet, took a few steps, and fell, rolling downward.

"Chris!" Barrigan shouted, reaching him and breathing heavily. "What happened?"

Chris looked up, in pain. "They . . . they

shot me. I was . . . I was offering myself as a h-hostage in Merilee's place. They agreed. Then . . . they shot me when I . . . started toward the house."

"Let me help you," puffed the mine-owner, pulling Chris to his feet. "I'll get you to Doc Rice's."

Lurching and stumbling, the two men descended the slope, then made their way along Georgetown's main street toward the physician's office. Citizens joined in to help and quickly learned the state of affairs at the big house on the mountainside. Word spread like wildfire through the town.

A few late breakfast customers were in the Alpine Café when an old man, obviously excited, came in and hurried to the counter. Jo-Beth Taylor was busy filling salt shakers.

"Miss Jo-Beth!" said the elderly man, his eyes wide.

"Goodness, Grandpa Kincaid," said the young blonde, "what are you all worked up about?"

The old man took a deep breath, swallowed hard, and said, "There's a gang o' killers up at Morey Barrigan's house. They're holdin' Dottie and them kids as hostages up there. They want the mine payroll and two hunnerd pounds o' gold!"

"Oh, Grandpa!" gasped Jo-Beth. "That must have been what Derek Sheffield came and got Dan about!"

"Yeah," replied Kincaid, "they've got him up there too! And . . . and Shirley and . . . and Merilee John. Chris just went up there to try and rescue Merilee, and they winged him!"

The few customers left their tables and gathered around the old man by the counter. Jo-Beth dropped a salt shaker. It bounced on the counter and fell to the floor, spilling salt in every direction. "They shot Chris?"

"Shot Chris!" echoed several of the customers.

"Yes'm!"

"Is he—"

"No, Miss Jo-Beth, he's still alive. Morey's got him over at Doc Rice's place right now."

"Is it bad?"

"I'm not sure how bad, honey," said the old man in a breathless voice. "There was lots o' blood!"

"And you say they have Dan up there as a hostage?"

"Yes'm," nodded Kincaid.

"Oh, dear," Jo-Beth said with a tremor. "Grandpa, you go back in the kitchen and tell Tinky that I've gone over to Doc's office. I'll be back in a few minutes."

Jo-Beth reached the doctor's office and pushed her way past the crowd that had gathered. Just as she reached for the knob the door came open and Morey Barrigan appeared. There was blood on his right hand and on his coat.

Instantly the crowd pressed him with questions about Chris John's condition.

"Doc says Chris will live, folks," he announced. "He's taking the slug out of him now."

"Praise the Lord!" breathed one of the women.

"Mr. Barrigan," spoke up Jo-Beth, "is it true they've got Marshal Starr up there?"

Barrigan frowned. "Yes. They've got him."

Jo-Beth's fingertips went shakily to her mouth. "What . . . what are you going to do?"

"Yeah, Morey," came an unidentified voice. "What are you goin' to do?"

Shaking his head, the mineowner ran a palm over his sweaty face. "I don't know. They've got the advantage on us. I've got to think on it."

"Well, while you're thinkin' on it,

Morey," chimed in a merchant named Bob Allen, "those dirty outlaws up there might shoot somebody else. I say let's all get our guns and storm the place!"

Allen's statement was met with an uproar of agreement among the crowd.

"No!" shouted Barrigan. "There's no way to take them by surprise. They'd kill everyone in the house."

"What do they want, Morey?" asked Dale Dixon, the town's clothier. He had arrived only moments before.

"They want the mine payroll that's due in here shortly," answered Barrigan. "They also want two hundred pounds of gold nuggets. Only there's a problem. I got a wire after the gang took the hostages. It was from the Kansas City bank. The payroll's being delayed. The Solomon River flooded in Kansas. Railroad trestle was damaged. It'll take a few days to repair it."

"Have you told the outlaws about it?" asked banker Carl Anderson.

"Not yet, Carl," replied Barrigan. "I was on my way up to talk to them when I heard the shots and found Chris wounded a few minutes later."

"I think we need to go up there with a show of force and let those stinkin' skunks know we mean business," the town black-smith said.

"Right, Jake!" agreed Bob Allen. "Best thing to do is go up there with an army and lay it on the line. Let them understand that if they harm those hostages, they'll all die!"

"Let's let Morey talk to them first," said Carl Anderson. "Maybe when they realize it will be several days before the payroll is going to arrive, they'll just take the gold and go."

There was a general agreement among the men that Morey Barrigan should parley with the outlaws. Not only were some of the leading citizens in danger, but their marshal was also at the outlaws' mercy.

"All of you go back to your work," said the mineowner. "I'll do everything I can to keep anyone else from being hurt."

As Barrigan turned and began threading his way through the crowd, Derek Sheffield arrived from the direction of the mine office. He waited until his father-in-law drew near, then said, "I just heard about Chris. Is he all right?"

Barrigan nodded. "Yeah. Doc says he'll make it. You take care of things at the office. I'm going up to try to reason with those vultures."

Within ten minutes Morey Barrigan reached the timber's edge, thirty yards from the house. Inching up behind a tree, he called out, "Musio! Tony Musio!"

"Who is it?" came the question from inside the house.

"Morey Barrigan! Salem said I should talk with you."

"You alone?"

"Yes!"

"If you're not Barrigan," shouted Musio, "there's a lot of lead coming your way!"

"I'm alone! Can we talk?"

"You got the money?"

"That's what I want to talk about!"

"Step out into the open!" shouted Musio. Barrigan left the shade of the trees and moved into the sunlight.

Remaining in the shadow of the door, Tony Musio said, "All right, Barrigan. That's far enough. Now, you got the money?"

Morey stopped. "Musio!" he called. "I want to know. Are the hostages okay?"

"Yeah," responded the swarthy outlaw. "Everybody's fine. But if you let anybody else come up here—"

Musio was interrupted by Merilee John,

193

who ran up beside him. "Mr. Barrigan!" she cried. "Is Chris all right?"

Angrily, Musio turned and shoved her across the room.

Feeling his utter helplessness, Barrigan said, "You don't have to treat her like that!" He could hear Merilee weeping in the background. Brett's voice rose, but his father could not make out what he said.

Anxious to quell Merilee's fears, Barrigan shouted, "Chris is okay, Merilee! You hear me? Chris is okay!"

Musio, still not showing himself, called out, "Hey, Barrigan! I asked you a question. You got the money?"

"There's a problem, Musio," said the mineowner. "The Solomon River flooded in Kansas. Train can't get through. Wire came a little while ago. Payroll won't be here for three, maybe four days!"

Musio swore heatedly. "I don't believe it, Barrigan! You're lying!"

"No, I'm not," protested the silver-haired man. "I'll get you the gold as soon as I can, but I can't do anything about the cash."

"What do you mean, as soon as you can?" bellowed the angry outlaw.

"We just shipped our gold to Denver,

Musio. It'll take at least another day to shake out two hundred pounds."

Musio's angry voice boomed, "You're stalling, Barrigan! You're going to get somebody in this house killed!"

Fear was evident in the mineowner's face. "No! I'm telling you the truth! You *must* believe me!"

Suddenly the door flew open. There was a slight pause. Then the blood-caked body of Barrigan's dog came sailing through the doorway. It landed on the edge of the porch. Momentum caused it to fall over, roll down the steps, and come to a rest on the rocky ground.

Barrigan's eyes bulged.

"I want that money *and* the gold by sundown, Barrigan!" bellowed Musio. "If I don't get it, it'll be the body of one of these hostages that'll be rolling toward you!"

Barrigan's voice choked with the tightness of sudden anger, unrestrained by fear. "Musio! I'd put it all in your hands if I had it! I warn you! If any of those hostages are harmed, this town will tear all of you limb from limb!"

"Sundown, Barrigan!" came the unwavering outlaw's response.

The door slammed.

Barrigan looked at Mutt's lifeless form lying at the foot of the porch steps. Strength seemed to drain from his body. Slowly he turned, shoulders drooped, and started down the steep slope.

X

Tony Musio stood in the door of the big house and watched as Morey Barrigan disappeared into the timber.

"What'll you do if Barrigan doesn't produce by sundown, Tony?" asked Hutch Reiner.

"I'll keep my word," the dark man said coldly. "We'll toss them a corpse."

The hostages looked at one another, fear on their faces.

"Morey Barrigan may be telling you the truth about the payroll," spoke up Dave Bradford. The blond man still lay in a prone position on the floor, a purple lump showing on his right temple, where Reiner had kicked him.

"You shut up, lawman," rasped Musio.

"Well, what if he is?" demanded Dave. "You're asking him to perform the impossible."

Tony's teeth bared. "I told you to shut up!"

"The man can't put money in your hands if he doesn't have it," said Dave heatedly.

Fury rising within him, Musio darted across the floor and drove a hard kick into Bradford's ribs. "I told you to shut your mouth, Starr!" he bellowed.

Instantly Shirley Sheffield sprang across the room like a cat. She was on Musio's back, raking his neck with her fingernails. Tony dropped to his knees, howling with pain. Reiner and Salem seized her quickly and pulled her off, each man gripping an arm. The gallant young woman struggled but could not break free.

Brett Barrigan leaped up, shaking his bandaged fists. "Let go of her!" he screamed.

Musio, back on his feet, whipped out his right-hand revolver and snapped back the hammer. Brett stopped in his tracks. The dark-eyed outlaw stepped to the youth and placed the muzzle between his eyes. Through gritted teeth Musio said, "I've been trying to decide whose corpse goes through that door at sundown, kid. You make one more foolish move and you're elected. Now go sit down."

Brett met the killer's gaze past the gun, then slowly backed away and took his seat.

Shirley, arms held tight by the two outlaws, glared at Musio. "You slithering snake," she hissed. "You're good at handling women and boys, aren't you? If I were a man, I'd wring your scaly neck!"

Dropping the pearl-handled gun in its holster, Musio stepped close to the angry woman and raised a hand to her face. Shirley's eyes showed no fear. Tony placed her cheeks between his thumb and fingers and squeezed, puckering her lips. "But you're not a man, honey," he breathed. "I noticed that right off." With that he bent down and kissed her hard.

Emily Barrigan watched as Musio kissed her sister repeatedly. Shirley made an agonizing sound deep in her throat, her eyes bulging. When Musio released her, she raised her knee savagely, catching him in the groin.

Tony howled with pain and doubled over. Reiner and Salem swung her around hard, slamming her against the wall. Musio, his face pallid, straightened up partially and glared hard at Shirley, one hand rubbing the scratches on the back of his neck. Suddenly his fist lashed out, striking her flush on the jaw. Shirley dropped to the floor like a soggy rag doll.

As the sun touched the mountains Morey Barrigan appeared at the edge of the timber, leading a horse bearing four sacks of gold nuggets. He called out, "Musio! Tony Musio!"

Inside the house the dark-eyed outlaw glared at Shirley venomously. She had come to and was tied in a chair. Jim Hicks, standing by a window, told Musio that Barrigan was at the edge of the trees.

The mineowner's voice cut the air again. "Tony Musio!"

Musio moved toward the door, still slightly bent from the kick to his groin earlier that day. Remaining just inside, he barked at the mineowner, "You got it all?"

Barrigan pointed to the four canvas sacks on the horse. "There's just over a hundred pounds of gold. It's the best I could do. It's a fortune, Musio."

"Where's the payroll?" demanded the outlaw.

"I told you. It's been delayed."

"You're lying!"

"No!" cried Barrigan. "If I had it, I'd give it to you!"

Musio's voice was high-pitched and angry. "I told you the payroll and two hundred pounds of gold by sundown, or somebody dies!"

"I did the best I could!" shouted Barrigan.

Musio turned and looked at Shirley Sheffield. A wicked pleasure flashed in his dark eyes. He walked toward her and stood, glaring.

"What you goin' to do, Tony?" asked Hutch Reiner.

"The old boy's probably tellin' the truth," said Musio. "But a little scare might make him hurry things along." Pulling one of his revolvers, he chopped the barrel hard against Shirley's left temple. As she slumped over he fired the gun into the floor.

Dottie Barrigan screamed.

Outside, the mineowner froze in fear. A minute later the screen door was flung open and the unconscious Shirley came hurling through the doorway. She rolled across the porch and sprawled, head downward on the steps.

Morey Barrigan stiffened in shock. "Oh, dear God! They've killed her!" he gasped.

While the stunned father eyed the blood on Shirley's face, Musio shouted at him from the doorway, "Okay, Barrigan, come get your daughter's body! Leave the gold on the steps!"

Barrigan stumbled up the incline, his mouth agape. Reaching the porch, he dropped the four sacks on the bottom step. Turning his attention to Shirley, he was surprised to see her still breathing.

Musio broke into a humorless laugh. "Scared you, didn't I, Moneybags?"

Barrigan said, "I hear you, but—"

"You'd better do it, bub!" cut in the heartless outlaw. "I'll give you one more day. But I promise—the next body dumped on the porch will be a dead one!" With that he stepped back and slammed the door.

Barrigan laid his unconscious daughter over the horse's back and headed quickly down the mountain. A large crowd was waiting at the bottom of the steep grade. Derek Sheffield shoved his way forward as people gasped Shirley's name. Someone shouted, "They've killed her!"

"No!" hollered Barrigan. "She's alive. They only slugged her!"

"What was the gunshot?" came an unidentified voice.

"It was just to scare me," he responded.

"I'll take her, Dad," offered Derek Sheffield, his face a white mask.

"It's okay, Derek," said Barrigan. "I'll keep her on the horse. Just run ahead and tell Doc Rice I'm bringing her."

Within five minutes the physician was washing Shirley's gash, preparing to stitch it up. He ordered Barrigan and his son-in-law to sit in the waiting room while he did it. The crowd outside had dispersed.

Sheffield looked shakily at his father-in-law and said, "Dad, I just don't know who could be giving out the payroll information. But you're right, it has to be someone here in Georgetown. I—" Just then Dr. Rice entered the room. "How is she, Doc?" he blurted.

"She'll be all right, son," said the elderly physician. "Took sixteen stitches to close up the wound. She's awake now. You and Morey may go in."

The doctor followed the two men into the room, closing the door. Shirley lay on a waist-high bed, gauze encircling her head. Derek stood on one side of the bed, Barrigan on the other.

Shirley focused on her father's face. With a faint smile she said softly, "Hello, Daddy." When her eyes found her husband's face, they went cold. The smile drained away.

Sheffield leaned over her and said, "Hi, sweetheart."

As he bent down to kiss her Shirley averted her head and spoke through clenched teeth. "Get away from me." Her voice was icy.

Sheffield swallowed painfully.

"Honey," said Morey, "what's the matter with you? That's Derek you're talking to."

Still refusing to look at her husband, Shirley hissed, "No. He's changed his name. It's Judas Iscariot."

Sweat beaded on Sheffield's brow. He could not bring himself to speak. Something turned in his stomach.

"Honey," said Barrigan, "what are you talking about?"

"He sold you out, Daddy. He's in league with those bloody thieves up there in the house."

Sheffield's eyes were closed. "No," he said weakly. "Shirley, how would you—"

"New card game at the Brown Palace, huh?" she interrupted.

Derek Sheffield knew he was caught. Tony Musio had double-crossed him. His face drained of color as he looked at Morey Barrigan.

"He set it all up, Daddy," said Shirley.

"Even putting the family in the fix they're in right now. It was his idea."

Sheffield's frightened gaze shifted from face to face. "No . . . I . . ."

Now Barrigan was boring him with angry eyes.

"Okay," said Sheffield, breathing unevenly. "Okay. I set up the payroll robbery. B-but this hostage thing . . . no. No, sir. I—"

"You're lying," rasped Barrigan, his face beet red. "I should—"

Dr. Rice stepped in. "Now, gentlemen," he said sternly, "this conversation is none of my business, but Shirley is. She's been through a lot today. This has got to stop."

Barrigan's face was like granite. Breathing out his words, he said, "If anyone up in that house dies, Derek, I'll kill you myself."

"Mr. Barrigan!" protested the doctor.

The muscles in Sheffield's face began to twitch. Nervously he touched Shirley's hand. "H-honey," he stammered, "I only d-did it f-for you. I wanted to g-give—"

"Get out of my sight," said Shirley, pulling her arm away. "If I see you in a thousand years, it will be too soon."

With his shoulders drooped, the guilty man turned slowly and walked to the door.

Pulling it open, he looked back at his wife and said, "I don't suppose it would do any good to say I'm sorry."

"Good-bye." Shirley's voice was hard, final.

Slowly he turned and left the room, closing the door behind him.

Barrigan shook his head, running his fingers through his hair. Dr. Rice busied himself making Shirley comfortable.

"I suspected him, honey," Barrigan said softly to his daughter. "He was the only person in Georgetown who had the payroll information. But I kept telling myself it just couldn't be true."

"I'm sorry, Daddy," Shirley said morosely.

"It's no fault of yours, honey," he replied. "But I don't know what I'm going to do about this horrible situation. There's no way I can hurry up the payroll shipment. My people in Denver will bring it just as soon as the train arrives, but the earliest I can hope for is the day after tomorrow."

"Maybe all we have is to stall them until then," said Shirley.

Barrigan sighed heavily. "I'm just afraid if I don't produce something by five o'clock tomorrow afternoon, they'll kill somebody."

XI

Just before sunup the real Dan Starr guided his black gelding onto Georgetown's main street.

Starr had been arrested by a posse from Rawlins, Wyoming, as the man who had robbed their town's bank. The sheriff had jailed him, not believing he had an identical twin brother who pulled the robbery.

Starr's only recourse had been to break jail, find Dave, and take him back to Rawlins. He had successfully managed to pry loose a window bar from his dilapidated cell, retrieve his horse and belongings, and had since trailed his twin to Georgetown.

Proceeding farther into town, Starr observed that only a few people were on the street. They were talking intently to one another. No one even noticed him ride in. Running his gaze back and forth, Starr sized up the town. He made note of the rickety miners' shacks along the river and the tent saloons scattered around.

The marshal's office came into view on the left. Then he spotted the Alpine Café.

His stomach growled as he swung from the saddle and wrapped the reins around the rail. Adjusting the twin Colts on his hips, he crossed the boardwalk and entered the café. Scanning the place, he noted that business was slow, a man and woman occupying one table.

The door to the kitchen came open. Starr's eyes took in a well-proportioned young woman, blond, arrestingly beautiful. A tray of freshly washed silverware was in her hands. When she saw him, the tray crashed to the floor. "Dan!" she cried. "How did you get away?"

The tall man stood there, stunned, as she rushed up and embraced him. "Oh, darling," she gasped, "I'm so glad you're safe!"

Before Starr realized what was happening, Jo-Beth Taylor stood on her tiptoes and wrapped her arms around his neck. She pulled his head down, and her lips came warm and soft against his own. Releasing him, she smiled through misty eyes. "I love you, darling. I'm so glad you're—"

Catching the surprise on Starr's face, the lovely young woman held him at arm's length and said, "Dan? Dan, what's wrong?"

Starr noticed that the two customers

were staring. A little Chinaman came from the kitchen, spied the silverware scattered on the floor, then focused on the tall man's face. "Ah, Marshal Starr," he said. "Velly glad to see you are okay!"

Within seconds Starr had the puzzle put together. For some reason Dave was impersonating him here in Georgetown . . . and he was doing it behind a marshal's badge.

"Dan?" Jo-Beth said again.

"Young lady," he said awkwardly, "I'm . . . I'm afraid there's been a misunderstanding here."

Jo-Beth blinked. "Dan, I—"

"I'm not who you think I am."

The young woman's mind flashed back to what Dave had said in the marshal's office just before their conversation was interrupted by Derek Sheffield. "Darling," she said hastily, "that's what you said yesterday when Derek came into the office. I'm a bit confused. I—"

"Young lady," he cut in, "I am Dan Starr. I just rode in here from Wyoming. Apparently my twin brother has led you to believe he is me."

Jo-Beth's mouth hung open.

"From what I can put together here," continued the tall blond man, "Dave has been impersonating me and for some strange reason is wearing a marshal's badge."

The Chinaman shook his head in disbelief and walked behind the counter to collect payment from the man and woman, who were about to leave.

Shock froze Jo-Beth's features. She seemed unable to speak.

"You said something about my getting away," said Starr. "You were glad I was safe. Is Dave being held captive somewhere?"

Her face colorless, Jo-Beth stammered, "I . . . I . . . f-feel a little weak. I think . . . I need to sit down."

Starr helped her to a table, pulled out a chair, and eased her into it. He sat down on the opposite side of the table. Tinky began picking up the scattered knives, forks, and spoons.

"You say your brother's name is Dave?" asked Jo-Beth.

"Yes."

"Then if you're the real Dan Starr, you'll remember me."

Starr's eyebrows arched. "We've met before?"

"I'm going to tell you where and when,"

said the woman. "If you're Dan Starr, you'll tell me my name."

Starr pushed his hat to the back of his head. "Fire away."

"Amarillo. Nine years ago."

The blond man studied her face for a long moment. "You're not . . . you can't be Sam Taylor's daughter! Jo-Beth?"

A smile spread over the woman's face. She nodded. "And you are the real Dan Starr."

"Yes'm. Boy, have you changed!"

"Dan, you never told us you had a twin brother."

Ignoring her statement, Starr said, "You were just a pug-nosed, freckle-faced kid. I never dreamed you'd turn out like this!"

Scarlet flushed her cheeks.

"How are your parents? Is your dad still punchin' cattle? Does your mother still cook like—"

"They're dead, Dan."

"Oh," said Starr, discomfited. "I'm sorry."

"You mustn't be," she replied. "There was no way for you to know. They were killed when a tornado caught them out in the open . . . nearly eight years ago." Reverting to the original subject, she said, "You never told us about Dave. Why?"

"It's a long story, Jo-Beth," he said. "But to be honest, I wasn't telling anybody about Dave back then, and I still don't. I'll explain later." He frowned. "Back to what I asked you a few moments ago—is Dave being held captive somewhere?"

"Yes," She nodded, her face pinched with worry. "A gang of outlaws is holding several hostages in Morey Barrigan's house up on the side of a mountain. Mr. Barrigan is the owner of the big gold mine here in Georgetown. Dan—I mean Dave—is being held as one of the hostages." She reached across the table and grasped his arm. "Oh, Dan, you've got to get him out of there!"

The tallman brought his gaze full on the lovely young woman. He carefully examined her worried face, like an Indian reading a sign. Quietly he said, "You're in love with that brother of mine, aren't you?"

Jo-Beth bit down on her lower lip. Tears welled up in her eyes. She spoke softly. "Yes. And he's in love with me." Looking down at the checkered tablecloth, she said, "Strange, isn't it? Here I thought I was in love with Dan Starr, and all the time I've been in love with his twin." Raising her eyes, she said, "But why would Dave Starr pose as Dan Starr?"

Starr's face went gray. This innocent trusting young woman had been taken in by the outlaw. She had to know the whole truth, sooner or later. Starr decided it might as well be sooner. It was going to hurt her, but there was no way to avoid it.

He spoke slowly. The difficult words came like pulling out deep-rooted stumps. "Jo-beth . . . his name is not Dave Starr anymore. He's using his middle name as his last name. He is now known as Dave Bradford. I don't know what he's doing wearing a marshal's badge. The man is an outlaw. Jo-Beth, I'm sorry, but—"

"No!" she said, standing up. Fixing her hot gaze on Starr's suntanned face, she said, "Do you know why your brother has been wearing a badge? I'll tell you why! A few weeks ago he took on the whole gang of bank robbers all by himself. He killed every one of them, Dan. Now why would a man who's an outlaw do a thing like that?"

"Well, I don't know, but—"

"He's a hostage right now because he was good enough to take the marshal's job. The bank robbers killed Marshal Plummer. Dan—I mean *Dave*—has been protecting this town until our new marshal gets here from St. Joseph, Missouri. If Dave was an outlaw, he wouldn't do that! He'd be on the run."

"Jo-Beth," said Starr, "I wish you were right. I wish Dave wasn't an outlaw. But in spite of all you've seen in him, he's wanted in Texas for bank and stagecoach robbery. They're after him also in Wyoming for bank robbery."

Jo-Beth pressed fingertips to her temples. "But he loves me, Dan. I know he does. Why wouldn't he tell me the truth? Why would he pretend to be you and—"

Dave's last words echoed in Jo-Beth Taylor's mind: *"Jo-Beth, I'm not . . . I'm not who you think I am."*

She collapsed back into the chair. Her eyes had a vacant, glazed look. "Oh, Dan . . ."

"What is it, Jo-Beth?"

"He . . . he tried to tell me. Something's been eating at him for a couple of days. Now I know what it is. He was trying to find a way to tell me his real identity. We were over in the marshal's office, alone. Dave was visibly upset. We were suddenly interrupted. But just before that, he said, 'Jo-Beth, I'm not who you think I am.' Do you see, Dan? He tried to tell me!"

213

Nodding, Starr said, "I'm glad for that."

Something else slid into Jo-Beth's memory. "Dan," she said. "Now I remember."

"What's that?"

"The day Dave rode into Georgetown."

"Yes?"

"He came in with the posse. They'd gone after the bank robbers . . ."

He waited patiently for her to collect her thoughts.

"The townspeople gathered in the street to look over the dead bank robbers. The posse started telling how the tall blond man had wiped out the gang single-handedly. Morey Barrigan asked the crowd if they knew who the man was. I spoke up and told everybody he was Dan Starr."

"I see."

"Later I found out that one of the men in the posse had identified him as Dan Starr before they rode into town. So you see, Dan, Dave didn't announce he was you. We made a mistake, and he just went along with it."

Starr fingered his chin thoughtfully. "Uh-huh. That's what happened, all right."

Jo-Beth laid her palms flat on the table. "I take it you're following Dave."

"Yes'm. But that story'll have to wait.

Right now I've got to find out the situation at the Barrigan house. I have to get Dave out of there."

Jo-Beth stood up and looked through the curtained windows toward the street. "I guess the whole town's probably gathering at the foot of the mountain this morning. You need to talk to Mr. Barrigan. He'll be with the crowd. Why don't you go over and wait at the marshal's office across the street? I'll run out and tell him you need to see him."

"No sense in you having to do that," said Starr, standing up and towering over her. "I'll go on out."

"I think it might be best if Mr. Barrigan sees you before the whole town does," suggested Jo-Beth. Suddenly spotting a young boy passing the window, she darted to the door and pushed it open. "Jimmy," she said. "Would you do something for me?"

"Sure will, Miss Jo-Beth. What is it?"

"Would you run as fast as you can to where the people are gathered at the end of town and tell Mr. Barrigan I need to see him right away? Tell him it's very, very important. I'll be at the marshal's office."

"Okay, Miss Jo-Beth," said Jimmy, and he took off quickly, heading up the street.

Leaving the café to Tinky, Jo-Beth crossed the street with the tall, broad-shouldered man. As they entered the marshal's office Starr said, "What are the outlaws demanding from Barrigan? Gold?"

"Yes. Two hundred pounds of it. Plus the mine payroll being sent here from Kansas City."

"It's not here yet?"

"No. It's been delayed because of a washed-out trestle in Kansas."

Starr laid his hat on the desk and sat down on a corner. Jo-Beth took a chair where she could see through a window and watch the street.

"How many in the gang?"

"I don't know," she replied, peering through the flyspecked window.

"How many hostages?"

"Five. Mrs. Barrigan, her teenage son Brett, her daughter Emily, and Merilee John, the Barrigans' maid . . . and your brother. Merilee John's husband went up there and tried to offer himself as a hostage in Merilee's place. They shot him. They also split open Barrigan's married daughter's head and let her go late yesterday afternoon."

"Did they kill Mr. John?" Starr asked.

"No. He's at Doc Rice's office. Word is that he'll be all right. Took the bullet in his left shoulder."

Starr shook his head. "I guess they mean business." After a brief pause he said, "Did they take over the house knowing the payroll would be delayed?"

"No. Word came on that after they were up there. The payroll was to be in by late yesterday afternoon."

"Have they been told about the delay?"

"I guess so. Mr. Barrigan went up there to tell them."

"So you don't know the situation at present?"

Jo-Beth shook her head. "No." Coming out of the chair, she peered through the window. "We're about to find out. Here comes Mr. Barrigan."

As the mineowner approached the door Jo-Beth moved into the opening. Dan Starr stood up.

Halting just shy of the doorway, Barrigan said, "What is it, Jo-Beth?"

"I've got a little surprise for you," answered the young woman. "Come in." As she spoke she stepped back.

Barrigan moved inside. His eyes locked

217

on the tall man's angular face. "Dan!" he gasped. "How did you get away?"

Before Starr could speak, Jo-Beth said, "This man is the *real* Dan Starr. The man we thought was Dan Starr is still up there in the house. They're twins."

The mineowner shook his head. "I've heard of identical twins, but this is uncanny. They're exact duplicates!" Extending his hand, he said, "I'm Morey Barrigan, Mr. Starr."

Starr met his grip.

"How do you happen to be in Georgetown at this time, Starr?" asked Barrigan.

"I've been trailing my brother," he replied.

"Oh, I see. And what's his real name?"

"Dave."

"What?"

"It's too detailed to explain now, sir. He goes by the name of Dave Bradford. He's wanted in Texas and Wyoming." Watching Jo-Beth from the corner of his eye, Dan said, "I've been mistaken for Dave by lawmen before. Not long ago he robbed a bank in Rawlins and hightailed it south, and a posse arrested me in his place. I broke jail to come after him. Got to take him back to Rawlins to clear myself."

Vexation showed in Jo-Beth's blue eyes. Visibly shaken, she moved to a chair and sat down.

Barrigan explained the circumstances up in the house to Dan Starr. He described the virtual fortification of the structure and its impregnable location.

"You've told them of the delay in the payroll?" asked Starr.

"Yep," replied the mineowner.

"And?"

"They're demanding both the payroll and the gold by sundown tonight," said Barrigan, his features haggard. "They think I'm stalling them. They don't believe the payroll's been delayed."

"How much is the payroll?" queried Starr.

"About a hundred nine thousand. We ship it in every three months."

Starr released a low whistle. "Certainly you stagger the dates of shipment, don't you?"

"Of course," said Barrigan flatly. "But the word on this one got out." He did not volunteer further information, though he assumed that word had gotten out, and like everyone else in town, Jo-Beth knew.

"How about the gold?" asked Starr. "Can

you show them good faith by producing their demands on that?"

Barrigan shook his head. "I took them half of it last evening. I'm going to do my best to have the other half ready by sundown. I've got my men working furiously on it. But even if we take them the other hundred pounds, I'm afraid of the consequences. Those outlaws are madmen, Starr. They've already killed my dog."

Jo-Beth jerked to attention. "They killed Mutt?"

Barrigan's lips pulled tight. "Yeah. They tossed his bloody corpse out the door. It will be the body of a hostage next."

Dan Starr instinctively felt for his guns. "Something's got to be done!"

Barrigan's voice was unsteady, and tears touched his eyes. "Will you help us, Dan?"

"I'm at your service," said the blond man.

"Good!" responded Barrigan. "First thing we need is lawful authority. We need another marshal. Will you take the job?"

"Jo-Beth says you've got a new one on his way. When do you expect him?"

"Any time now. Will you wear our badge till he gets here?"

"All right," said Starr.

The town council's chairman stepped to

the desk and pulled open a drawer. He produced a badge and, holding it in his hand, swore in Dan Starr as Georgetown's interim marshal. "I think it would be best," he said, "if we let everyone think you are your brother. We'll tell them you were able to break away from the outlaws up at the house. It'll save a lot of explaining for now."

Barrigan asked Jo-Beth if anyone had heard the conversation between her and Dan Starr as to his identity. She told him that a man and a woman had been in the café when Starr had come in, but they were travelers just passing through town. The only other person was Tinky. She would see that he kept it to himself.

A crowd was gathering outside the marshal's office, to see what the mineowner would do next. Barrigan said, "Let's go out, Dan. We might just as well tell them right now that you escaped from the house. We'll say we're trying to come up with a plan to get the hostages loose."

The two men stepped out on the boardwalk. The crowd was stunned to see their marshal. Barrigan did most of the talking and quickly convinced them that Dan Starr had escaped but hadn't been able to get anyone else out with him.

Merchant Bob Allen spoke up from the crowd. "There's only one way to handle this as far as I'm concerned, Morey. Let's arm ourselves to the teeth and go up there!"

"Yeah!" shouted Alf Boggs. "Let's go take those hostages away from them!"

There was instant response from the crowd. "Let's go!" they shouted.

"Wait a minute!" bellowed Starr above the roar. "Those outlaws have all the advantages. That house is a fortress. They could kill some of the hostages before you got through the door."

"Sounds to me like they're goin' to start killin' them anyway, Marshal!" shouted Jake Gibbs, the blacksmith.

"We've got to negotiate for whatever time we can buy," said Starr.

"Morey already tried that," parried Bob Allen. "The only thing to do is jump them!"

"What if it was *your* family up there, Bob?" snapped Jo-Beth Taylor, who now stood beside Dan Starr. "You'd feel different about it then!"

"The first thing to do," said Starr, "is wait until sundown and take them as much gold as possible. They'll at least know Mr. Barrigan is trying to cooperate."

Reluctantly the crowd gave in to Starr's

reasoning. But the new marshal knew if the outlaws rebelled, the citizens of Georgetown were going to get out of hand.

As the crowd was breaking up, the Wells Fargo stage rolled into town and halted in a cloud of dust. A strange rectangular black box rode overhead in the rack.

XII

Dick Lang, the Georgetown Wells Fargo agent, stepped off the boardwalk to meet the Denver stage. As passengers alighted, Lang spoke to the driver and shotgunner. "Hey, boys, what you got up there? Looks like a coffin!"

"That's exactly what it is," said the driver. "It should have been here several days ago, but it got shoved into a back room in Denver when it was taken off the Kansas City train. The agent suddenly remembered it was there. Imagine forgettin' about the coffin!"

"Corpse in it?"

"Nope," answered the driver. "The thing's empty. It's addressed to your new marshal, Dan Starr."

Nearby, Dan Starr and Jo-Beth Taylor

stood in front of the marshal's office, talking to Morey Barrigan, when two of Georgetown's citizens came down the street carrying the black coffin. One of them called, "Present for you, Marshal!"

Starr's gaze swung to the pair and the dismal object they were bearing. "Did you say that thing was for me?" he asked.

"Yes, sir," came the reply. "Tag here says this coffin is for Marshal Dan Starr, Georgetown, Colorado. Says it's to be opened only by you."

"It can't be for me," said Starr. "There's no way—" Suddenly he realized it was for Dave.

Jo-Beth gasped, the realization striking her also.

"How heavy is it, fellow?" asked the tall man.

"Feels like it's empty," said one.

"Take it in the office," Starr said, gesturing toward the door.

Jo-Beth and Barrigan followed Starr and the black coffin inside. Starr instructed the two men to place it on the floor. Dick Lang had given one of the men a slip of paper for Starr to sign. As the men left, Starr rummaged through the desk and found a screwdriver.

Jo-Beth leaned over and read the tag aloud: 'Marshal Dan Starr, Georgetown, Colorado, to be opened only by addressee." She shuddered. "What kind of weird madman would send a person such a thing?"

"Don't know," replied Starr, dropping to his knees beside the coffin.

Morey Barrigan stood over Starr while he used the screwdriver as a crowbar and worked the lid loose. Jo-Beth watched in suspense as he laid down the tool and pulled back the lid. A single white envelope lay on the bottom. One word was written on it: *Starr*.

Opening the envelope, Dan Starr stood up. He unfolded the sheet of paper and read the message to Jo-Beth and the mineowner:

Starr—
You killed my brothers. I'm going to kill you. Got it from an eyewitness. Jake tried to surrender, and you shot him anyhow. I'm coming after you. I'll see to it you die a slow, agonizing death. You won't know when or how, but you'll die soon. When you're dead, I'll bury you in this coffin. Sweet dreams.
Curwood

Raising his gaze to Barrigan, Dan Starr said, "This has to refer to the incident when Dave took out the gang by himself."

Barrigan nodded. "It does. There were two Curwoods in that bunch."

Starr's eyes widened. "The Kansas Curwoods!"

Barrigan nodded again. "Your brother killed Jake and Brant Curwood, Dan."

Starr's brow knotted. "But how would whichever Curwood brother this is know that Dave killed them . . . or that he'd be come marshal of Georgetown under my name?"

"There's only one answer to that," Barrigan said grimly. "It was the same snake in the grass who tipped off the outlaws about the payroll shipment. It was my son-in-law, Derek Sheffield. He's been working with them all along. It's his fault my family and those others are hostages up there in the house right now."

Jo-Beth said, "Morey, I'm so sorry."

Starr shook his head in disbelief at what humans could do.

"Read me that part about the eyewitness again, Dan," said Barrigan.

Raising the paper, Starr read aloud, "Got

226

it from an eyewitness. Jake tried to surrender, and you shot him anyhow."

Barrigan's face reddened. "That's a lie! There were no eyewitnesses! When the posse rode on to the scene, Jake Curwood was already dead. Nobody saw Dave shoot the kid. Dave told me he tried to get the kid to surrender." Shaking his head, he said, "It looks like Derek was even trying to get your brother killed."

Jo-Beth's brow furrowed. "Morey, wouldn't all of this have to be done by telegraph?"

"Yes."

"Then Clarence Sheets is involved."

"Yes. I'll have to deal with him later. Right now there are more important matters."

Jo-Beth nodded. She turned to Dave's brother. "Dan, have you ever seen any of the Curwoods?"

"No, ma'am."

"Then whenever this killer hits town, you won't know what he looks like."

"That's right." The blond man nodded.

"I could let you look at the wanted posters," said Barrigan, "if that would be any help. But from what I've heard, the brothers don't bear any strong resemblance. Jake and Brant certainly didn't look alike."

Jo-Beth's face went white. "This leaves you totally defenseless, Dan. Strangers are in this town all the time. It could be one of those men that got off the stage today."

"Ironic, isn't it?" said Barrigan. "Your outlaw brother did something good, and it still puts you on the spot."

Starr chuckled dryly. "Even if I tried to convince this Curwood brother that the man who killed Jake and Brant was my twin, he wouldn't believe me."

"Guess not," said Barrigan. "You *are* Marshal Dan Starr."

"Then you've got to leave here at once!" said Jo-Beth breathlessly.

"Can't do that," responded Starr. "My brother is up there in Mr. Barrigan's house. I have to deliver him safely to Rawlins. And I can't leave those other folks in the hands of killers."

Jo-Beth stared pensively at the floor. Without looking up, she said, "Dan, when you turn Dave over to the authorities in Wyoming . . . how long do you think he'll be in prison?"

"I don't really know," replied the tall man. "He's wanted in Texas too. 'Course, he did just clean up on the gang that robbed the bank here in Georgetown. That'll go in his favor." Starr rubbed his square jaw. "Might be they'd give him ten years. Maybe less."

Jo-Beth did not hesitate. "Whatever it is," she said evenly, "I'll wait for him."

There was a long moment of silence, then Starr said, "Jo-Beth, honey, you'd best forget my brother as quickly as possible. You're only asking for a big load of troubles."

"It isn't possible," she retaliated firmly. "I love him, Dan. I don't care what he's done. Down inside, he's sweet and good. I'll wait for him, no matter how long it has to be."

"I'll say one thing," mused Starr as he eyed the street through a dirty window. "My brother is a mighty lucky man to have a woman like you loving him."

Jo-Beth blushed, a demure smile parting her lips.

Starr turned to Barrigan and said, "I'd like to go up there and look the situation over, if you don't mind."

"Sure." The mineowner nodded. "But don't let them see you. I'm the only one they'll talk to. If they see you, it could go bad for those in the house."

"I understand," said Starr. "I'll stay out of sight. Just want to get an idea of the layout."

Barrigan excused himself, saying he needed to check on how the men at the mine were coming with the gold.

Jo-Beth was left alone with Dan. Studying his face, she asked, "Do you have any idea how you're going to get Dave away from those outlaws?"

"Not really," he answered. "If they leave with him as a hostage, I'll have to trail them and try to cut him away from the others, which will be difficult. But if we're unable to stop them up at the house, that's the only choice."

Jo-Beth was thoughtful for a moment. Then she said, "Dan, would you do something for me?"

"Of course."

She slipped behind the desk. Rummaging for a moment, she pulled an envelope and a piece of paper from a drawer. "I want you to give something to your brother for me. Since we have no way of knowing how things will go with these outlaws, you might be a long way from here when you get to . . . get to see Dave."

"It's a possibility," he agreed.

Hastily Jo-Beth wrote on the paper. When she was finished, she wrote *Dave* on the envelope. Before folding the sheet, she said, "I would like you to read this."

"But it's for Dave," he said, eyeing the envelope.

"Yes, but I want you to read it so if something happened to the note, you could tell him how I feel."

Dan hunched his shoulders and took the paper from her hand. He was touched deeply as he read it.

My darling,
As you read this you will be aware that I know Dan Starr is your twin brother. I know your name is Dave Bradford and that you are wanted by the law. Dan has told me that he must take you to the authorities in Wyoming in order to clear his name. You will be sent to prison.

Please understand this. I did not fall in love with a name. I fell in love with a man. You. I will wait for you, my darling. My love is yours. I care not what you have done. I ony know that you are a good man—a kind, tender, gentle man, whom I love very, very much.

Please come back to me, Dave.

Yours always,
Jo-Beth

Dan blinked against the moisture gathering in his eyes. Folding the paper, he placed it in the envelope. Then folding the envelope, he stuffed it into his shirt pocket and said, "My brother is a mighty fortunate man. I will do my best, Jo-Beth, to see that you get to tell him in person."

Derek Sheffield had spent a miserable night. After leaving the doctor's office, he had not known where to turn next. He could run, but where to? And what would he do once he got there? Unable to come to a decision, he had curled up in a corner of a shed at the edge of town, but sleep had eluded him.

Hatred raged in him toward Tony Musio. The dark-eyed outlaw had double-crossed him. He had told Shirley of his own part in the plot to steal the payroll and the gold. That meant one thing—that Musio had already planned to cut him out of the take. And he had laid his job and his reputation on the line to set up the whole operation. Musio was planning to ride off and leave him holding the bag. An *empty* bag.

232

Not only were his job and reputation gone—so was his marriage. Shirley would never forgive him. His children would grow up to despise him. He could never face the Barrigan family again, let alone the people of Georgetown. His life was a shambles. He had no more reason to live. For that, he decided, Tony Musio was going to pay with *his* life.

Sheffield left the shed and moved quietly through the town, murder burning in his heart. Slipping along alleys and staying in the shadows of buildings, he spotted a horse tied to a hitching rail, a Winchester rifle in the saddle boot. When no one was looking, he grabbed the rifle and ducked back out of sight. Finding the gun fully loaded, he headed toward the Barrigan house on the side of the mountain. As he neared the other edge of town his mind burned with one thought—how to kill Tony Musio. One thing he knew for sure: Periodically, every-one in the house had to come outside to use the privy. That included Tony Musio. When Musio came out the next time, he was a dead man.

As he sneaked past the crowd gathered at the bottom of the steep grade, Sheffield heard the people talking excitedly about the fact that Marshal Dan Starr had somehow managed to escape from the outlaws up at the house. He was at the marshal's office with Morey Barrigan right now. Sheffield swore under his breath. By now Starr would know the whole story. Barrigan had done nothing but make threats so far, but sooner or later he would have the marshal arrest him. He would go to prison. Bitterness claimed him as he realized that his greed had placed him where he was now and that instead of gain he had lost everything dear to him.

Topping the grade, Sheffield moved through the deep shadows of the trees. He had been there twenty minutes when he saw D.J. Salem leave the house and go to the privy, which was located a few dozen yards to the west. Not long after Salem returned to the house, Brett Barrigan appeared, escorted by Mike Poston.

Sheffield's breathing grew hot. "Come on, Musio," he said in a whisper. "Come out where I can get a bead on you."

Dan Starr hurried past the crowd of townspeople gathered at the bottom of the path to the Barrigan house. They were wide-eyed and eager, wanting to see something done

234

right away. Several men approached him as he strode past, asking what he was planning.

"Can't tell you right now," he said. "You'll all just have to be patient. The lives of the hostages are at stake."

Unknown to Starr, and unnoticed by the crowd, Jo-Beth Taylor also slipped into the shadow of the trees, following the same route up the mountain that Derek Sheffield had taken a little while earlier. She had to find out what Starr was going to do once he had seen the layout of the house and surrounding area. The man she loved was in that house.

As Starr was nearing the top he happened to look behind him and saw Jo-Beth duck behind a tree. When she looked around to see if he had spotted her, he had pulled into the shadows and was looking straight at her. Quickly she ran to him.

"Jo-Beth!" he breathed. "What are you doing here?"

"I just had to come," she said in a whisper. "I've got to know what you're going to do. I want Dave out of there."

Starr swung a glance up toward the house. They were some thirty yards from the clearing. "You wait here," he told her firmly.

"I don't want you anywhere near where you can get hurt or get taken as another hostage."

Jo-Beth nodded, leaning against the tree.

Starr hastened upward.

Nearby, Derek Sheffield was peering around a tree, watching Jim Hicks and Al Craig come out of the house and head for the privy. Suddenly he heard someone behind him. At the same instant that he whirled, Dan Starr saw him. Sheffield thought the marshal had come to arrest him.

In his panic, he said, "Get away from me, Starr! You're not taking me!"

Hicks and Craig wheeled toward the outburst, drawing their guns. Starr saw the outlaws, whipped out his guns, and fired a split second before they did. Hicks and Craig went down, their own bullets going wild. In the same split second that Starr was gunning down the outlaws, Derek Sheffield swung his rifle around and fired. Dan Starr dropped to the ground. Jo-Beth came on the run, screaming at Sheffield that Starr had not come to arrest him and asking him to help pull Starr out of sight from the house.

Bewildered and confused, Sheffield took hold of Starr and dragged him into the thicket. He could hear other outlaws gathering around Hicks and Craig, swearing. They were hurriedly dragging them into the house, not knowing how many men might be out in the trees.

Jo-Beth knelt beside Dan Starr. Sheffield's bullet had hit him square in the chest. He was barely conscious. "Dan! Dan!" she cried. Turning her scornful eyes on Sheffield, she hissed, "You filthy animal! Haven't you done enough? Did you have to shoot him? He saved your life! Those two men would have killed you! Get out of my sight, you Judas! You dirty traitor!"

Derek Sheffield stood up. His eyes seemed to lose focus. While Jo-Beth attended to Dan Starr he disappeared into the trees.

Jo-Beth soon saw there was nothing she could do. The pallor of death was on Starr's face. "Oh, Dan!" she gasped, seeing the blood spread around the hole in his shirt.

"Jo-Beth," he said weakly. "Do . . . do you really think . . . Dave could . . . go . . . go straight?"

"Yes," she nodded. "I really do. There is so much good in him."

"If . . . Dave will promise you that . . . he'll walk straight, Jo-Beth . . . tell him . . . tell him I said to . . . marry you as Dan

Starr. Let the world think . . . it was . . . Dave Bradford who died."

Dan Starr closed his eyes. His head fell to one side, and his breathing ceased.

Weeping, Jo-Beth pulled the folded envelope from the dead man's shirt pocket. There was blood on it. Blinking against her tears, she turned and walked down the path slowly, clutching the bloodstained envelope.

XIII

When Jim Hicks and Al Craig were dragged into the Barrigan house, Tony Musio was ready to start killing hostages. Craig was already dead. Hicks lived long enough to tell the others that there were only two men out in the trees. One was Derek Sheffield. He could not identify the other one, who was still in the shadows when he started shooting. It was the man in the shadows who had gunned both him and Craig.

Musio's wrath cooled somewhat when he realized that Sheffield had probably acted without Barrigan's knowledge, apparently bringing along a friend. No doubt he was furious that Shirley had been told he was in league with the robbers. Musio now realized that he had made a mistake in alienating Sheffield, but he reasoned that Sheffield would be a hunted man and would not dare hang around for long. The dark-faced outlaw shrugged off this setback and ordered Reiner and Salem to drag the bodies outside, onto the back porch.

It was nearly noon when Nelson Blechman stirred from his position by a front window. "It's Barrigan," he announced.

Morey Barrigan called out from the edge of the trees, asking to speak to Musio. When the outlaw leader appeared in the doorway, Barrigan said, "Musio, you have to understand something. I did not order Sheffield to come up here! He did that on his own! We're looking for him now. You haven't hurt somebody because of it, have you?"

"Naw," replied Musio. "I figured that's what it was. That son-in-law of yours is a little miffed at me. I think you have better sense than to risk getting anyone in here killed."

"That's right," confirmed Barrigan. "I'm doing everything that I can to meet your demands."

"Good," responded Musio. "Then you're goin' to have the payroll and the gold ready by five o'clock." It was a statement, not a question.

"If the payroll's here by then, you'll have it," the silver-haired mineowner replied. "If it's not, I'm no magician. There's nothing I can do about it."

"There'll be a corpse on your hands if you don't!" bellowed Musio. "I want two horses up here by four o'clock. One is for your marshal. I want another one for one of your family to go along when we leave here. You hear me? *Horses* at four! *Gold* and *payroll* at five!" With that he disappeared from the door.

Because Musio had called the man inside the house "your marshal," Barrigan knew that none of the outlaws had seen Dan Starr's face clearly in the shoot-out earlier. He turned and headed down the mountain.

When Barrigan arrived back in town, he saw Jo-Beth Taylor standing apart from the crowd that had gathered, trying to get his attention. She and Barrigan had agreed not to reveal for the moment that Dan Starr had been killed. His body was still up on the mountain, and people assumed their marshal was watching the house.

Weaving through the crowd, Barrigan made his way to the young blond woman.

Guiding him away from earshot of the others, she said, "Morey, you've got to come with me to Shirley's house. She asked me to come and get you."

"What is it?" he queried.

"I think you'd better see for yourself," she replied.

Barrigan and Jo-Beth ran together in the direction of the Sheffield house. As they turned the corner and headed down the street, Barrigan was surprised to see his daughter, her head bandaged, standing in front of the house. She was waiting for them.

Gasping for breath as he drew up, the mineowner asked, "Shirley, what is it? You should be resting in bed."

Shirley's face was pale, her features stoical. Her lips were thin and colorless. Looking at her father with half-vacant eyes, she said, "Come with me, Daddy."

Jo-Beth followed as Shirley led her father to the back of the house. Moving into the shadow of a large cottonwood tree, she stopped. Looking quizzically into her impassive eyes, Barrigan said, "Honey, what is it?"

Without speaking, Shirley slowly raised a hand and pointed up into the tree. Morey

Barrigan's heart seemed to freeze. His mouth worked, but he could not find his voice.

Dangling overhead by a long rope encircling his neck was Derek Sheffield. His face was bloated and gray-blue. The soft breeze that worked its way through the branches caused the body to sway slightly.

Barrigan brought his gaze back to Shirley. Tonelessly and bereft of emotion, she said, "Tony Musio was right. Derek was a Judas Iscariot. He even chose to die like Judas."

Inside the Barrigan house Tony Musio moved back into the parlor, pulled out his right-hand revolver, and checked the loads. He noticed that Emily Barrigan was watching him. When their eyes met, a tentative smile touched her mouth. The handsome outlaw grinned boyishly. He gave the pearl-handled weapon a half spin, adeptly tossing the barrel up and over in a backward flip that brought it neatly in line with the holster. The shiny metal smoothly vanished into the dark leather.

Emily smiled again.

Dottie Barrigan's face reddened as she noticed her daughter's behavior. Without speaking, she glared at the girl angrily. Emily ignored the glare.

"Well, ladies," said Musio, "looks like we're going to be your guests till five o'clock. How about hopping out there to the kitchen and rustling us up some grub? Hutch, you keep an eye on them."

Dottie turned to Merilee John, who now bore a large purple mark on her face. "I guess we'd better do it," she said with resignation.

As Merilee rose, Dottie said to her daughter, "Come, Emily. Let's fix all of us something to eat."

Emily rose reluctantly. Walking past Tony Musio, she gave him a quick, flirtatious look. The dark man's eyes sparkled.

Dave Bradford, still flat on the floor and tied securely with a rope, had witnessed the exchange. "You leave her alone, Musio."

Musio gave the bound man a narrow-eyed appraisal. "You're not in much of a position to do anything about it, now are you, lawman?"

"She's a decent girl," rasped Dave. "Stay away from her."

"She likes me." Musio grinned. "Can I help it if females find me irresistible?"

"I find you irresistible too," Dave said malevolently. "If I could get my hands on you, I wouldn't be able to resist breaking your neck."

The outlaw laughed. "You'll have to break those ropes first!"

In the kitchen the three women began preparations for the meal. Hutch Reiner sat at the table, chewing tobacco as he watched. Rattling pans, Dottie moved up beside Emily and whispered, "You stop it right now! Do you hear me?"

Without whispering, the girl replied with a giggle, "Stop what, Mother?"

Dottie's eyes were hot as she hissed, "Playing up to that man who beat your sister and shot Chris John!"

Emily giggled again, tossing a glance through the door to where Musio stood. "But Tony's a handsome man, Mother," she said, smiling. "He's a real he-man. A girl doesn't find that kind very often."

Dottie's mouth dropped. "Emily Barrigan! I don't know what's gotten into you! I've never seen you like this before!"

At the table Hutch Reiner chuckled, then spit tobacco on the floor.

"I never met a man like Tony before," retaliated the girl, throwing another glance toward Musio.

Merilee John spoke up, a note of disgust

in her voice, "Emily, your mother's right. You shouldn't have anything to do with that outlaw."

"It's none of your business," Emily countered caustically.

"That's right!" said Tony Musio, who had moved to the kitchen door. "It's none of your business, lady."

Dottie wheeled, anger livid in her face. "Well, it's *my* business," she snarled. "You stay away from my daughter!"

Musio threw up both palms. "Don't bust an artery, ma'am. All we did was smile at each other."

Dottie turned red with indignation, glared at Emily, then returned to her work. Emily sneaked Musio another smile and attended to her own task. Musio grinned and returned to the parlor. Hutch Reiner chuckled as he took it all in.

Later, Nelson Blechman ate his meal while standing guard at the window. The others sat with the hostages around the big kitchen table. Under the fiery glare of Dottie Barrigan, Tony Musio sat next to Emily. Brett Barrigan's bandaged hands made him clumsy with the fork. Dave Bradford remained on the parlor floor, his empty stomach complaining at the aroma of hot food.

Merilee John could see Dave's prone form through the doorway. Appealing to Musio, she said, "You're not going to let Marshal Starr go hungry, are you? He didn't get any breakfast."

Swallowing a mouthful of potatoes, Musio said, "Yep. Lawmen ain't human. They don't need to eat."

Brett Barrigan had been picking at his food. Looking across the table at Musio, he said crustily, "You won't eat when you get to hell either."

The outlaw leader's eyes burned red. Standing up, he threw his chair back and snatched Brett away from the table. Dottie cried out in fear. Musio slammed Brett to the floor and pulled his right-hand gun. Cocking the hammer, he pressed the black muzzle between the youth's eyes. Breathing hotly, he hissed, "You'll go to hell ahead of me, smartmouth! Know any prayers?"

Dottie cried out, "Please! Don't kill him!"

"Shut your trap, woman!" snarled the outlaw, holding his eyes on Brett.

Merilee took hold of Dottie, squeezing her tight.

Speaking to Brett again, Musio said, "I asked you if you know any prayers, kid!"

Brett was speechless.

"Don't know any, eh?" chortled the dark-skinned outlaw. "Well, let me see now. Maybe I can say one for you: Now I lay me down to sleep. A bag of peanuts at my feet!"

D.J. Salem snorted through his nose and broke into a hearty laugh. "Hey, that's pretty good, Tony! A bag of peanuts at my feet!" He laughed harder.

Brett Barrigan was numb. He had not known human beings could be so callous and cruel.

Ejecting a coarse laugh, Musio stood up and slid his gun in its holster. "One more word out of you, kid, and you're dead, do you hear me?"

Brett nodded wordlessly.

Dottie and Merilee eyed each other, faces blanched. Emily showed no emotion.

After the meal was over and the kitchen cleaned, Musio had everyone gathered once again in the parlor. He sat down in an overstuffed chair and looked at Emily, who sat across the room with her mother and Merilee John. Merilee was expressing her concern about the condition of her husband and Shirley Sheffield.

"You better worry about yourself, lady," D.J. Salem said to her. "You might be the one to die if that payroll ain't here by the deadline."

Merilee threw him a look of contempt and went silent.

"Which one we takin' with us, Tony?" queried Reiner. "I mean other than the blue-eyed lawman here."

Musio's dark eyes fired on Emily Barrigan.

"Oh, no, you don't!" cried Dottie. "You're not taking her!"

"Now, Mother," said Emily softly, "it's better that I go than someone else. Tony wouldn't hurt me, would you, Tony?"

"Stop it, Emily!" said Dottie curtly.

Musio grinned recklessly. "No, miss. I wouldn't hurt a pretty little thing like you." Extending a hand, he said, "Come here."

Dottie Barrigan was turning red again. "You stay where you are, Emily!"

"Oh, now Mother," said Emily, rising. "It's not going to hurt anything for me to go over there and sit by Tony. You worry too much."

Tears filled Dottie's eyes as Emily crossed

the room and settled demurely on the arm of the overstuffed chair. Musio smiled when the girl slid an arm around his neck.

"Oh, Emily," sobbed the despondent mother, "what's happening to you?"

While Dottie buried her face in Merilee's shoulder, the latter looked at Emily and said angrily, "Isn't she going through enough without you acting this way? What's got into you, Emily? You've never been like this before."

Squeezing the dark-haired outlaw's neck, Emily said with soft defiance, "I've never met a man like this before."

Mike Poston laughed and scratched his heavy beard. "Looks like your charms have really worked on this one, Tony!"

Musio chuckled and squeezed Emily's hand. "Well, when a man is gifted, it's just there."

Emily giggled, squeezing the outlaw's shoulders.

At four o'clock Morey Barrigan led two horses past the big house and placed them in the corral just outside the barn. When he had completed the errand and left, Tony Musio spoke to his companions. "I'm going out to the corral and look those horses over."

"Wait a minute, Tony," spoke up Hutch Reiner. "It'll be five o'clock in less than an hour. We need to have an agreement on what we're goin' to do if Barrigan don't have that payroll."

Musio's eyes roved over Dottie, Merilee, and Brett. "We'll kill us a hostage," he said, and shrugged. "Emily and the lawman are going with us, so it'll have to be one of these three."

Standing by a window, rifle in hand, Nelson Blechman said, "Well, let's decide right now which one it'll be. I got a feelin' there ain't goin' to be no payroll."

Musio hitched at the low-slung guns on his hips. He pursed his lips in thought. "Make them draw straws. The one with the short straw dies if Barrigan shows up without the payroll."

Reiner guffawed and strode to the kitchen. Pulling three straws from a broom, he broke them into different lengths. He then placed them in his big, meaty fist so that the exposed tips were even. The secret of their lengths was hidden behind the pudgy fingers.

When the big man returned to the parlor, the faces of the three prospective victims were pale with fear. Emily stood next to

Tony, whose dark features showed amusement at seeing them cower.

"Okay," said Reiner, approaching the two women first. "Take your pick."

Dottie Barrigan swallowed hard and said, "There's . . . there's no need for this. If you're going to do this awful thing, just let it be me."

Tears filled Merilee's eyes. Half crying, she said to Musio, "How can you be so inhuman? Do you have no conscience at all? None of us—"

"Shut up!" barked the outlaw. "Now, nobody's pulling any heroics, Mrs. Barrigan. You draw a straw. You, too, Mrs. John."

Emily stood there watching, her face showing no emotion as her mother and Merilee reached shakily toward Reiner's outstretched hand.

Each pulled a straw, neither looking to compare them. Reiner then moved to where Brett sat near the broken window. The youth looked up at him blankly. "No matter which straw I get," he said in a level tone, "I'm the one you should kill."

"I said no heroics!" snapped Musio.

Brett Barrigan stared at the outlaw with narrowed, defiant eyes.

"Don't push him, Brett," said Dave

251

Bradford from his prone position on the floor. "He'll kill you now and kill one of the women at five o'clock."

"That's sage advice, blue eyes," said Musio. "You picked the thoughts right out of my brain." Turning back to Brett, he said, "Take your straw, sonny."

The youth reluctantly accepted the remaining straw from Reiner's hand. Holding it up in his bandaged hands, he said, "I think this is the short one."

The two women examined their own straws. Merilee's was shorter than Dottie's, but Brett's was the shortest. The frantic mother began to sob.

"No need to bellow, Mrs. Barrigan," said Musio. "If your husband comes across with the payroll, the brat will live." Swinging his gaze to the clock over the mantel, he said, "We've got forty minutes. I'm going out and take a gander at those two horses."

As the outlaw turned toward the door, Emily touched his arm. "Tony?"

"Yes, Emily?"

"Could I walk with you?"

The outlaw ran a finger over his dark, thin mustache. "Sure, you can, honey." Speaking to his companions, he said, "Don't none of you boys bother us, you hear? I mean it. We'll be back shortly."

Dottie screamed, "Emily! You stay in this house!"

"Mother," Emily said coolly, "we're only going to look at some horses."

With that the couple moved out the door. Emily walked beside Musio, clinging to his arm as they stepped off the porch. "Tony," she said, "when you take me out of here, can I stay with you?"

Smiling at the girl with false affection, he said, "You mean permanent?"

"Mmm hmm."

"Sure, honey," he lied.

As they made their way to the corral Tony Musio veered close to the edge of the cliff. The wind plucked at the dark locks on his hatless head. Taking Emily's hand tightly in his own, he stopped and peered over the edge. "Long way down, isn't it?"

"Daddy says to that first rock ledge down there it's four hundred feet. From there to the bottom of the canyon it's another three hundred."

Musio stepped away from the edge, shaking his head. Releasing Emily's hand, he walked briskly to the two saddled horses at the corral gate. Carefully he went through the saddlebags and checked the cinch straps. Emily walked idly along the cliff's edge. She swung her gaze northward, looking down at the town. The roar of the river met her ears, mingling with the whistle of wind. *From up here,* she thought, *the town looks so peaceful. No one would know of the turmoil it's experienced in the last few days.*

Satisfied with horses and gear, Musio returned to where Emily stood. They were just out of sight of the house, the corner of the barn blocking the view. Taking the girl's hand, he pulled her closer to him, away from the cliff edge. He said, "Did you really mean what you said about never meeting a man like me before?"

Emily laid both palms on his chest and tilted her pretty face upward. "Yes," she breathed, lowering her eyelids.

When their lips met, the girl slid her hands around to his back as he folded her into his arms. She kissed him softly, warmly. Just as Musio released her and smiled, Emily snatched his left-hand revolver from its holster and jumped back, out of his reach. At the same time she cocked the hammer, holding the weapon steady with both hands.

Musio's eyes popped. "Girl, what in the—"

Emily's face was rigid. Lips pulled into a

thin line, she snapped, "Reach down real slow now. Take the butt of the other gun by your fingertips and lift it out. Drop it on the ground."

"Emily, what are you doing?" he gasped. "I thought—"

"You thought wrong!" she snarled. "You never attracted me for one minute, you filthy, blood-hungry rat! I'm sorry I had to kiss you to get this gun, but I'll wash my mouth off later."

Musio stared down the black barrel of his own revolver. Emily did not waver. There was a determined look in her eyes, an unyielding set to her jaw. His mind raced for a solution.

The girl had wisely backed up two more steps. The edge of the cliff was ten feet to her left. . . .

"What are you going to do?" asked Musio, stalling for time.

"*You're* going to climb over the edge of that cliff," said Emily. "While you hang on with your fingertips, you're going to call your henchmen out here and tell them to throw their guns into the canyon."

The swarthy outlaw began shaking his head. "Girlie, you're crazy if you think I—"

Emily raised the ominous, dark muzzle,

lining it between his eyes. "You'll have a chance to live only if you do what I tell you. A bullet through the bridge of your nose will end it all. Now quit stalling. Lift that gun out with your fingertips!"

Tony Musio was a man noted for being fast on the draw. Instantly he made up his mind that he was not going to dangle from the edge of a cliff. His hand darted downward for the gun in the holster. Adeptly Emily lowered the muzzle and pulled the trigger. The gun bucked against her palm as it roared. The bullet ripped through Musio's right thigh. He dropped to the ground, grasping the wound and yowling in pain.

Quickly Emily snatched the other revolver from his holster and stood over him. She threw a glance over her shoulder toward the house. Though she and the outlaw were not visible from there, Emily expected to see Musio's partners coming around the barn on the run. She waited a long moment while Tony writhed in pain on the rocky ground. Still no one appeared.

Throwing the second weapon over the cliff, she cocked the other and stepped close. Aiming it directly at his head, she said levelly, "Okay, get your carcass over the edge."

Gritting his teeth in pain, the outlaw gasped, "You can't do this!"

"I can put lead in your head, just like I did in your leg," warned Emily.

The look in her eyes told Musio that Emily meant business. Grunting and gasping in pain, he crawled toward the rocky edge. There was a trail of blood on the hard surface behind him. Reaching the edge of the wind-swept precipice, he looked up at the stern-faced young woman. "Please, Emily," he pleaded, tears in his eyes. "Don't make me do it."

"Your friends can pull you back up after all their guns are pitched into the canyon. You just grab the edge and hang on." Motioning with the gun in her hand, Emily commanded, "Over the side. Now."

The resourceful girl glanced again in the direction of the house as the wounded, sobbing outlaw bellied down and swung his legs over the rocky ledge. He wrapped both arms around a jagged outcropping and dangled there. Still none of the gang had put in an appearance.

Musio could feel the blood running from his thigh. Frightened, he clung hard while his body dangled in the wind. "Emily!" he cried. "I can't hang on very long! I'll bleed to death!"

"Then you'd better start calling them quick," Emily said, aiming the gun at his head. "One at a time. Start with the one called Hutch. When he shows, tell him to throw his gun over the cliff and lay down on his belly."

The dark-eyed outlaw looked up at her helplessly.

"Well, go on," she snapped. "Call him."

"Hutch!" bellowed Musio. *"Hutch!"*

Within twenty seconds the big stoop-shouldered man lumbered around the barn, revolver in hand. When his eyes flashed the message to his brain, he stopped dead in his tracks, mouth agape.

"Tell him!" commanded the determined girl, her hair flying in the wind.

Musio, the flesh of his hands and fingers white against the sharp rocks, shouted, "Kill her, Hutch! Quick! Kill her!"

Reiner lifted the muzzle of the gun upward, but Emily's was already aimed. She fired, hitting the big man dead center in the chest. Reiner's body jerked, then flopped to the ground. The gun tumbled from his fingers. Still alive, he rolled over, rising to his knees. His last effort was to reach for the gun. Emily waited, her own weapon trained on the mortally wounded man.

Reiner's trembling fingers touched the cold grip of the revolver. Emily was about to shoot him again when he fell flat and lay still. Though he was ten yards away, she could tell he was dead.

Musio was struggling, trying to raise himself from the cliff's edge. Emily swung around, her face livid with rage. Pointing the threatening black muzzle at his head, she hissed, "Kill her, huh? Do you know how to pray, Musio?"

The outlaw's face was a leaden mask of fear. Drops of cold sweat stood out on his forehead. He could not speak.

"Come on, big man," taunted Emily. "You said a prayer for my brother. Can't you remember it? Only it's not a bag of peanuts at *your* feet, buster. It's four hundred feet of space!"

Suddenly Nelson Blechman and Mike Poston came around the barn on the run. They saw the lifeless form of Hutch Reiner on the ground, fingers outstretched for the gun. They looked down to see the jagged edges of the cliff's rim. Musio's hands and forearms were clearly visible. Emily's gun was aimed at him.

For a moment the two outlaws froze.

"Throw your guns in the canyon!" barked Emily. "I'll kill him if you don't!"

Half crazed with terror, Musio screamed, "Kill her!"

Instinct raised Nelson Blechman's weapon. Emily swung her gun toward him. Both guns fired at the same instant. The girl's bullet dropped Blechman in his tracks as she took the outlaw's slug in her side.

Mike Poston got off a shot at Emily that whined over her head as she fell flat on the cliff's edge. Still conscious, the girl saw Poston bend over Blechman. Musio was grunting, straining, trying to pull himself up. The gun was still in Emily's hand. Quickly she reached out and hammered Musio's fingers savagely with the barrel.

Emitting one wild scream, the swarthy outlaw released his grip and fell from view.

Poston heard the fading scream as Musio plummeted downward. He ran to the rocky ledge, his complete attention on the place where he had last seen Musio. Then he looked at Emily, who lay motionless on the hard surface. She was not breathing. Her eyes stared sightlessly into space, and spots of blood showed on her side. The bearded outlaw leaned over the windy precipice and let his gaze fall four hundred feet downward. Tony Musio lay in a grotesque, crumpled heap on the jagged ledge far below.

Hastily Poston returned to Nelson Blechman. The man was dead. He hurried toward the house.

D.J. Salem dashed out on the porch, saying, "What happened?"

"That girl got hold of Tony's gun," gasped Poston.

The hostages, filled with fear, rose to their feet as the two outlaws came through the door. Dave looked up from the floor.

Dottie choked. "Where's my daughter? What happened out there?"

Poston was answering Dottie's questions, but he spoke to D.J. Salem. "Tony's dead. So's Hutch, Nelson, and the girl."

Brett and Merilee grasped Dottie as her legs turned to rubber. Quickly they guided her to a chair.

"Tony told us not to bother them, but we should've gone out there when we heard that first shot, D.J.," said Poston. "Somehow the girl got one of Tony's guns from him and shot him. Must've been in a leg. Then I guess she made him crawl over the rim of that cliff out there and hang on to the edge. She shot Hutch, and when we got there, she was holdin' a gun on Tony while he was hangin' on for dear life."

"Mom, did you hear that?" cried Brett. "Emily was stringing Musio along. She was setting him up!"

"Oh, dear God, forgive me!" sobbed Dottie.

"Who killed the girl?" asked Salem.

"Nelson did," came Poston's quick reply. "They both fired at the same time."

Dottie wept bitterly, asking her dead daughter to forgive her.

"We've got to get out of here," breathed Poston. "They'll hang us for sure for killin' the girl. Let's go!"

D.J. Salem and Mike Poston took the four sacks of gold, retrieved their own horses, and rode quickly off the mountain. They angled away from the rutted road halfway down, galloped along the edge of the river, and disappeared in the timber, heading south.

When the two outlaws had galloped into the timber, Dottie turned to her son and said, "Brett, untie the marshal. I'm going to find Emily's body."

Merilee was on Dottie's heels as she moved through the door. As the two women were halfway across the yard they saw a small form step around the corner of the barn. Holding her side and partially doubled over, she said, "If you're looking for a corpse, Mother, you're in for a disappointment."

"Emily!" shouted the shocked mother. Bounding to her daughter, Dottie wept and said, "They told us you were dead!"

"Let's get her into the house," said Merilee, taking hold of the wounded girl. "She's bleeding."

"I don't think it's too bad, Mother," said Emily as they eased through the door into the parlor. "Let me just lie down on the sofa."

Merilee helped Emily onto the sofa.

"Oh, Emily," cried the regretful mother, kneeling beside her, "I know now what you were doing. I'm sorry for the things I said and for what I was thinking about you."

"It's all right, Mother," said the girl, clutching her bleeding side. A weak smile curved her lips. "I really made you believe I'd gone bad and fallen for Tony, didn't I?"

"Yes, honey," admitted Dottie, "you certainly did. You convinced everybody, including Tony."

"It was the only way I knew to get close

enough to one of his guns," said the girl, wincing.

"Well, you did it, Emily," said Dottie. "You did it, and now they're gone."

Looking her mother straight in the eye, she said, "What about it now, Mother?"

"What about what?"

"Do you think I have acting ability?"

Dottie almost laughed despite her tears. "There's no doubt in my mind, honey. You are without question a great actress!" Quickly Merilee took scissors and cut away the cloth from around the wound. It brought relief to Dottie to see that it was only a flesh wound. The bullet had passed through cleanly.

When the wound had been washed and bandaged, Dottie asked, "Emily, what made Poston think you were dead?"

"I told you, Mother, I'm an actress. When he came close to look at me, I held my breath and stared vacantly into space."

Dottie wept with joy and hugged her daughter.

XIV

Dave Bradford stood in the funeral parlor, somberly staring down at the lifeless form of his twin brother. With the help of Georgetown's undertaker, Dan Starr's body had been smuggled in so that no one in the town was aware of it.

Jo-Beth Taylor stood at Dave's right side, her shoulders slumped. On his left was Morey Barrigan.

"I'll form a posse, Dave," the mineowner said. "We'll go after the other two. Oh, by the way—Carl Anderson told me a while ago that Jim Stokes did a hurry-up job on your bounty money. The four thousand is waiting for you at the bank."

Dave turned slowly and said, "You mean I can still collect it?"

"Sure. Why not?"

"Even when you know I'm a wanted man?"

Barrigan gripped Dave's upper arm. Looking at him solemnly, he said, "Your past doesn't count here. I don't care what you were. I have seen what you for what you *are*. You're the best marshal this town ever had. If I hadn't already hired Todd Daley, I'd ask you to stay on as our permanent marshal."

Dave grinned broadly. "There's nothing I'd like more, if it were possible."

"You understand, I couldn't turn Daley away now."

"Oh, that's not what I meant, Morey," Dave said softly. "I meant that there are lawmen looking for me. There's no way I could be any town's permanent marshal."

Gazing up at the tall man, Jo-Beth said, "Could I ask you something?"

Dave could hardly look her in the eye. "Sure."

"You were going to tell me who you really were yesterday morning, weren't you?"

"Yes, I was," he said, tight-lipped.

Jo-Beth's eyes misted. "Dave, you really want to walk straight with the law, don't you?"

"I'd give my right arm if I could undo the past and start over."

A smile graced the young woman's beautiful lips. "Well, you can, Dave. You can start over, and even keep your right arm."

"I don't understand."

"Before Dan died, Dave, he left a message for you. Part of it is this: He said, 'If Dave will promise you that he'll walk straight, tell him I said to let the world think it was Dave Bradford that died.' "

"Think about it, Dave," said Barrigan. "Your brother has given you a chance to start over. Nobody in this town knows there were twins except Tinky at the café, the undertaker, Jo-Beth, and myself. Both Tinky and the undertaker have sworn to keep it to themselves. We'll give Dan a very private burial, and you can be Dan Starr for the rest of your life."

The possibility of it hit Dave like a blow. His heart pounded in his breast as he pondered on it while gazing for a long time at the body of his twin brother. Then he pulled the sheet over the lifeless face. "All right," he said, looking at Jo-Beth. "From here on out I'm Dan Starr."

Jo-Beth flung her arms around him. Barrigan shook his hand and said, "Well, *Dan*, will you stay on as Georgetown's marshal until Daley arrives?"

"I sure will!" came the new Dan Starr's reply.

"Good! I'll gather a posse. We'll go after those two outlaws."

"Look, Morey," said Dave. "Let me go

267

after those two outlaws myself. I can handle it faster than a posse can. I'll get your gold back for you. Besides, you need to be up at the house with your family."

Barrigan considered it for a moment. "Okay," he said. "You're the man wearing the badge. How soon will you pull out?"

"Soon as I can pick up a rifle at the office and a little food to take along."

"All right." Barrigan nodded. "I have no question you can bring in a mere two outlaws. Go to it!" He grabbed his hat and was out the door.

Jo-Beth walked beside the new Dan Starr as he headed for the marshal's office. "Dave—I . . . I mean *Dan*," she said. "Oh, I don't know what to call you."

"After the way I've deceived you, Jo-Beth," he said ashamedly, "there are probably some choice names you'd like to call me."

"But I don't feel that way," she replied, touching his arm. "I love you."

"Honey," he said as they entered the marshal's office, "you were in love with the other Dan Starr. I was a fraud."

Pushing the door shut, Jo-Beth said, "No, darling. I was, and still am, in love with *you*."

Dave's heart thumped in his chest. Looking deep into her dark-blue eyes, he said, "Do you really mean it?"

Jo-Beth produced a bloodstained envelope from the pocket of her gingham dress. Extending it to him, she said, "I gave this to your brother to give to you. It was in his pocket when he was shot. Please read it."

He took it and opened the envelope. Jo-Beth watched his pale-blue eyes moisten with tears as he read the letter. When he had reached the last word, he wrapped his arms around her, holding her close. "I have no idea what I'm going to do or where I'm going to go, honey," he half whispered.

"Whatever or wherever, I'll be with you," she breathed.

The couple enjoyed a long, lingering kiss, then he said, "What was the other part?"

"Of what?"

"My brother's message. You said there was more to it."

"Oh," Jo-Beth said, her face tinting. "Well . . ."

"Come on."

"Well . . . he said . . . he said you should marry me as Dan Starr."

Cupping her lovely face in his hands, he asked, "*Will* you marry me as Dan Starr?"

Weeping, Jo-Beth threw her arms around his neck. "Yes! Oh, my darling, yes!"

The new Dan Starr kissed her again. The sound of Denver's stagecoach rumbling to a halt out on the street met their ears.

Dan said, "We'll have the bounty money to start on, honey. I have to go after those outlaws now. We'll make plans as soon as I return."

At that instant a knock sounded at the door. It came open, and a stockily built man said, "Marshal Starr?"

"Yes," responded the blond man.

"I'm Todd Daley."

"Oh, sure!" Dan smiled, shaking his hand.

Dan introduced Jo-Beth and quickly filled in the new man on what had happened in Georgetown. He then explained that he was about to go after the two outlaws.

Adam Curwood felt displeasure to hear that so many of his men were dead, but now he had in his grasp the man who had killed Jake and Brant. Vengeance would soon be his. While Dan pulled a rifle from the rack and picked up a box of cartridges, Curwood eyed the black coffin sitting in the corner. "You collect those things?" he asked.

"Long story," said Dan. Morey Barrigan

had already shown him the coffin and the threatening letter.

"Look, Starr," spoke up Curwood, "how about me comin' with you?" To Curwood this would be the perfect opportunity to kill Dan Starr, plus catch up to his two men who had the gold.

"Morey Barrigan will have to swear you in," said Dan. "Besides, you must be tired from your trip."

"I'm fine," responded Curwood. "And as prospective marshal I think it's my duty to help you bring these men in and recover the gold."

"Okay," said Dan resignedly. "We'll rent you a horse at the livery. Morey can swear you in when we get back."

Jo-Beth said, "I'll pack enough food for both of you, Dan. Come by the café before you pull out."

The young woman hurried to the café while the two men went to the livery. Twenty minutes later Jo-Beth handed a heavy knapsack to the man she loved, as he sat his horse beside Todd Daley, in front of the Alpine.

"You be careful, Dan," said Jo-Beth. "I feel better since Marshal Daley is going with you."

Dan leaned from the saddle and lifted the blond woman to him with an arm around her waist. After kissing her soundly, he said, "I'll be back."

Ready for the black coffin, Adam Curwood thought smugly.

"I love you, darling," whispered Jo-Beth.

"I love you too," he replied, kissing her again. Easing her to the ground, he said, "Honey, will you get word to Morey that Mr. Daley has arrived and that he's gone with me?"

Jo-Beth assured the man she loved that she would get the message to Barrigan.

The two lawmen rode out of town. As they reached the edge of the timber Dan pulled his horse to a halt and twisted around in the saddle. Jo-Beth stood in the dusty street, watching him. The wind toyed with her long blond tresses in the light of the reddening sky. She lifted her hand to wave. Dan waved back, then spurred his horse into the trees.

The two outlaws had left a trail that was easy to follow. The lawmen rode hard, trying to use what daylight was left. Adam Curwood was thinking about how to make Dan Starr suffer before he died.

Long shadows closed around them as

272

they threaded their way southward. The gigantic mountains loomed on all sides, thrusting their jagged peaks upward, touching the darkening sky.

As the first evening star glittered faintly between two towering summits to the west, a small herd of mountain goats darted across the riders' path and flitted into the dense forest. Somewhere nearby a stream gurgled.

The last rays of light were fading when they rode into a small clearing surrounded by a thick tangle of trees and brush. "Looks like a good place to camp," said Dan. "Darkness has about got us."

Adam Curwood nodded and dismounted.

"I think we gained on them," Dan said, following suit. "We might be close enough that we'd give ourselves away with a fire. Better eat cold supper tonight."

"Outlaws probably won't build a fire either," said the imposter. "How far do you figure we've come from town?"

"Probably seven or eight miles," Dan replied.

The gusting wind caught the tree branches overhead, making them creak and groan.

Curwood sat down on a rock and looked up at Dan Starr's outline against the evening sky. A silent rage flared within him.

He envisioned the fateful moment when his little brother faced this man's guns and tried to surrender. He could see Starr standing over Jake, muzzles smoking . . . the boy shot through the head.

The rage inside the outlaw turned cold as he studied the tall man. A knot of icy hatred formed in the pit of his stomach, sending shivers through his veins. Loathing filled his eyes. But Adam Curwood was in rigid control. *Tomorrow, Starr,* he thought. *Tomorrow you pay!*

Suddenly gunshots echoed across the dark mountains, followed by the roar of a huge cat. Then came the screams of men mingled with the angry cry of the cat. There were two more shots, another scream, then all was quiet.

The sounds were not far away, due south.

Looking in that direction, Dan said, "Somebody's run into a cougar, Daley. Could be our men. We'd better investigate."

Curwood agreed, and the two men mounted their horses.

After riding only fifteen minutes, they came upon a large clearing. Giant rock formations girded the area. Horses nickered at them from a thicket of trees. Sliding from his saddle, Dan said, "Have your gun ready,

Daley. I'm going to gather some sticks and make a torch."

Within minutes Starr struck a match and flared the dry sticks in his hand. The leaping flames revealed two bodies sprawled within a few feet of each other. It took Curwood a few seconds to recognize D.J. Salem and Mike Poston. He breathed a silent oath as Dan said, "It's the outlaws, Daley!"

Curwood's features went white when he inspected the meaty mass where Mike Poston's face used to be. The outlaw leader waited at the edge of the ring of light as Dan knelt down and said, "These boys had a confrontation with a cougar."

Curwood let his gaze settle on the lifeless form of D.J. Salem. The entire front of Salem's body, including his face, had been mauled savagely.

Still kneeling, Dan said, "Well, our search is over. The gold will be in their saddlebags." Standing up, he used his torch to follow the path of blood that led into the woods. "That beast is still alive," he said, pausing near the edge of the trees. "It'll be back. Pity the man who has to face it."

Slowly slipping the revolver from his holster, Curwood stepped quietly toward the blond man. Dan's sixth sense suddenly came to life. He turned to see the big iron coming down in a violent arc.

Metal met flesh with a sodden sound. Dan saw thousands of swirling stars as the ground rose up and hit him in the face. The whole world seemed to spin. He raised up on his knees, then an inky black pit opened up and he seemed to fall in.

XV

Dan Starr opened his eyes and blinked. Dawn was lighting the world around him. Quickly the realization came over him that his hands were tied behind his neck and his ankles were bound together. He was lying on his side.

Pulling his knees up, he rolled to a sitting position. His head felt like something had exploded inside it. Batting his eyes against the growing light, he tried to focus them on objects around him. Abruptly Dan's heart froze in his breast. Not twenty feet away the black coffin rested in a quiet, foreboding manner on the ground. A wagon and horse team stood near.

From behind, a malevolent voice cut

the air. "Well, Starr, for a little while there I thought I had hit you too hard. Would be a pity for you to die that easy."

Slowly the owner of the voice walked in front of the blond man, a rifle in his hand. Frowning up at him, Dan said, "Daley, what on earth are y—"

"I'm not Daley!" growled the outlaw.

Dan's eyes flashed back to the black coffin. Like a gust of cold winter the truth came home. Lips pulled tight, he said, "What did you do with Todd Daley, Curwood?"

"Shot him in the head," replied the vengeful man coldly. "Dumped his miserable carcass off the train into the Solomon River."

Dan looked at the coffin, then ran his gaze to the wagon.

"You've been out quite a spell, Starr," said Curwood. "I rode to town, busted the hostler over the head, and stole the wagon. Didn't take much to break into your office and get the coffin."

"What now?" asked Dan flatly.

Curwood laughed fiendishly. "You were right. That cat my boys wounded is still alive. And he did come back. I shot at him a couple times—not tryin' to hit him,

277

of course. But he knows what a gun is, since last night. He'll be back again. I'm saving him for you." The venomous outlaw laughed again. "Or should I say, I'm savin' *you* for *him?*"

"You're crazy," Dan said.

Curwood leaned close. "Am I? That cat was wounded by humans on this spot last night. He's interested in killing humans on this spot. My gun has held him at bay. You won't have a gun, Starr. Just like Jake didn't have one when *he* died."

The outlaw pressed his face close to Dan's, his breath hot and foul. "You killed my baby brother after he threw down his gun and surrendered."

"I suppose Derek Sheffield told you that," said Dan. "Well, he lied. He wasn't there at the time. I tried to take Jake alive. He swung his gun on me."

Ignoring Dan's explanation, Curwood said coldly, "Now, the first thing you're going to do is dig your grave. Then I'm going to fix you up so that cougar can have a little fun. When he's clawed you to death, I'll kill him, and bury you nice and neat in the coffin."

Curwood had placed the black coffin where the earth was relatively soft in the clearing. He untied the tall man and, keeping a gun on him, put a shovel in his hands. As Curwood made himself comfortable in the shade of a lone pine tree ten yards away, rifle across his legs, Dan Starr pitched dirt while the sun rose higher in the Colorado sky.

The sun was midway in the morning sky when Jo-Beth Taylor stepped out of the general store with a small sack of groceries in her hands and started toward the Alpine Café. Just then a buckboard wagon pulled up, and she recognized the driver as a woman from one of the outlying ranches.

"Hello, Melinda," she called, walking up to the wagon. "In town to do some shopping?"

"Why, yes, Jo-Beth," Melinda replied. "And I thought I'd stop in at the marshal's office to see if Todd Daley had arrived yet. My husband and I knew him before we moved to this area." She laughed lightly. "Let me tell you, that tall drink o' water will be surprised to find out we're his new neighbors."

Jo-Beth smiled at the woman. "I'm sure he will, but the surprise will have to wait a bit. Mr. Daley and the former marshal are trailing some men south of here." Jo-Beth nodded good-bye and started to turn away, but then her brow furrowed and she looked back at the woman. "Melinda," she said slowly, "did you say that Todd Daley is tall? I mean real tall?"

"Why, yes."

"You mean he isn't about five nine, five ten, and built broad and thick?"

Melinda giggled. "Not at all. Todd is six feet five, and quite slender."

Jo-Beth thought of the threatening note that lay in the bottom of the black coffin. Suddenly she knew that Dan Starr was out there in the mountains with the man who had come to kill him. Quickly excusing herself, she darted down the street toward the doctor's office. Melinda called out to her, but Jo-Beth was totally absorbed by the awful truth that had just hit her.

Doc Rice and the Barrigan family were gathered in the inner office when Jo-Beth charged through the door. Shirley was seated between her parents, and Brett stood next to Emily's bed, holding her hand.

All eyes turned to the intruder, who spoke frantically to Morey Barrigan. "We've got to do something! The man we thought was Todd Daley is the killer who sent the black coffin!"

Dan Starr stood in the open, his hands lashed behind his back. A long lariat rope was tied around his waist, knotted at the small of his back. The other end of the rope led to the lone, slender pine tree near the center of the clearing.

The diabolical Curwood stood before Dan, rifle in hand, laughing. "Well, Starr, if you can move fast enough, there's thirty feet of rope. You ought to be able to outrun the cat. If not, maybe you can kick him to death!" Laughing again, he pointed to a tall rock formation some fifty yards east of the clearing. "See that rock? I'm going to sit up there and watch the show."

The cry of the wounded cougar was definitely on its way back to the camp. The second cry had been much closer than the first.

Curwood vanished into the timber to begin his climb. Dan nervously ran his gaze over the area. The black coffin sat forty feet away, neatly parallel to a six-foot-deep rectangular hole. The pile of dirt was heaped on the opposite side. Nearby lay the grotesque bodies of the two dead outlaws.

Dan's head jerked around sharply. The pained wail of the incensed cat pierced the air, echoing simultaneously off the walls of the stone-slabbed mountains. His spine went cold, and sweat beaded on his brow. He had faced death more times than he could count, taken chances that normal men would consider foolhardy . . . but this was something else.

He swung his eyes back to the mangled bodies of Salem and Poston. Digging in for traction, he pulled hard against the rope that squeezed his slender waist. It was no use. His eyes moved to where the rope was tied around the tree. He could clearly see the knot, but Curwood had placed it high up on the trunk, out of the reach of his tied hands. Bowing his shoulders, he wrenched his wrists savagely against the cords, until his muscles ached and the flesh was raw. Then, to his surprise, he felt something give. He went through the same motions again, but to no avail. There was no question though—the cords were definitely looser. The cry of the crazed beast split the thin mountain air again. This time it was even closer.

As Dan continued to wrestle against the binding on his wrists, Curwood called from his perch high on the rock formation. "He's comin', Starr! Think about Jake and Brant! If you'd let them live, you wouldn't be in this fix! It's your own fault!" His words were followed by an evil laugh that echoed across the rugged land.

Suddenly, a hundred yards away, a flock of birds took flight from the trees. The cougar howled again.

Dan's hands and wrists were bleeding. He felt a cord slip over the heel of his right hand. There was more room yet!

"Get ready, Starr!" came Curwood's fiendish voice.

Dan could feel his whole body trembling. Feverishly he labored, sensing more loosening of the cords. Again the animal wailed. With the sound of flapping wings another group of birds abruptly headed skyward. The horses were nickering nervously.

The tall man felt his right hand come loose behind his back just as the hissing cougar stepped out of the shadows on the south side of the clearing, twenty yards away. Its brownish-yellow coat was splotched with blood along the left side, where it had been shot by the escaping outlaws.

The huge beast paused and surveyed the scene. Curwood was silent now, his attention on the cougar. Dan stood as still as possible, working with his free hands on the knot at the small of his back. The cat gave no sign that it had seen Dan.

Emitting a vicious hiss, the cat moved smoothly to the grave and looked into it. It sniffed the coffin, hissed again, and moved toward the corpses of the outlaws. While the curious animal slinked slowly from one body to the other, Dan backed cautiously toward the tree where the lariat was tied. He had undone the knot at his waist but knew that to turn and run would be suicide. Any lateral movement would draw the beast's attention. Hoping Curwood's eyes would be on the big cat, he darted his hands from behind his back and quickly tied a slip knot, forming a loop in the end of the rope. He had used a lariat expertly in his ranching days.

Suddenly the wild, wounded cougar lifted its head and stared straight at the tall man. It showed its fangs, hissed, and letting out a violent wail, charged.

Curwood had been staring at the cat with fascination. He laughed gleefully as the cougar charged.

Dan waited till the last split second, leaped aside, and flung the loop over the animal's head. Giving the lariat a quick jerk, he tightened the loop. The cat whirled with a deep-throated growl. Dan darted in the direction of the black coffin as the cat lunged. The cougar hit the length of the rope. The impact spun him around by the neck.

From the top of the rock the furious outlaw leaped up, unable to believe his eyes. Dan Starr had freed himself and roped the cougar. *"No!"* Curwood cried. "No! No!"

The cat hit the end of the rope again. Dan looked across the clearing to where his horse was tethered in the trees. He could make a dash for it, but Curwood would be able to get off two or three clear shots at him. He had decided to try it when the huge animal lunged and hit the end of the rope the third time. Dan saw the broken knot whirl around the tree. The cougar was free but didn't know it. The next lunge would tell it.

Thinking fast, Dan ran to the coffin, flipped up the lid, climbed in, and pulled the lid down. He quickly found that the crosspieces on the inside made good handles. Gripping hard, he braced himself for the animal's next move.

From up on his rock Curwood watched the angry cougar lunge again. This time the rope on his neck trailed behind, like a dead snake.

Curwood was almost immobile with fury. He could easily have shot Starr at any moment, but he didn't want it to end so easily. He watched the cat approach the coffin warily, sniffing along the edges. From inside Dan peered through the tiny horizontal crack around the lid. The fangs and wirelike whiskers were plainly visible.

High up, the raging outlaw screamed, "No! No! Come out of there, Starr! Come out of there!"

Curwood knew Dan would stay in the coffin as long as the cat was there. Almost insane with the thwarting of his plan, he worked the lever of the rifle. He would drive the cat back. Starr must come out and take his medicine. Shouldering the weapon, he put a bullet near the front paws of the cougar. The animal bounded away, dragging the rope.

"Come out of there, Starr!" the outlaw bellowed.

The coffin lid did not move. Curwood shouted again, commanding his prisoner to get out of the black box. Wild with anger, the outlaw began scrambling down the steep formation, scattering rocks.

Within one minute Curwood's feet touched the level ground. He started for the coffin when he heard the maddened cougar howl from the deep shadows off to the right. Turning, he saw it charge. Quickly Curwood raised the rifle and fired point-blank. The cat screamed, did a somersault . . . then lay still.

With his eyes bulging like a madman, the outlaw wheeled and faced the coffin. "All right, Starr!" he yelled. "I'll do the cat's job!" He fired the rifle into the coffin. A bullet hole appeared instantly, exposing the wood's light color. Working the lever and pulling the trigger as fast as he could, Curwood emptied the rifle into the coffin.

His insane laugh echoed through the surrounding forest. Throwing down the rifle, he whipped out his pistol and screamed, "How do you like it, Starr? I told you I'd put you in there! Here's some more!"

While the outlaw insanely fired shot after shot into the black coffin, splattering splinters in every direction, he did not notice the cougar stirring. His first bullet had only grazed the wild animal's head, momentarily stunning it.

Curwood's hammer was slamming on empty chambers repeatedly when he became aware of the cat's wild cry. Wheeling around, his face froze in stark terror as the beast charged. He did not even have time to reach for his derringer. A helpless wail escaped his lips just before the cougar struck. His attempt to fight off the angry cat was futile. One mighty paw raked his head, twisting and snapping his neck. Screeching and hissing wildly, the cougar tore the outlaw's body to shreds.

Suddenly, from the north side of the clearing, three rifle shots rang out in rapid staccato. The huge cat fell dead on top of Curwood's mangled, bloody corpse.

Rifles smoking, Morey Barrigan, Brett Barrigan, and Bob Allen nudged their horses forward. Their eyes scanned the area, searching for Dan Starr.

Brett's gaze fell on the bullet-riddled coffin. "Oh, no!" he gasped.

"What is it?" his father asked. Sliding from the saddle, the youth replied with shaky voice, "The coffin, Dad. Looks like Curwood put him in there, then . . ."

Bob Allen dismounted, swearing.

Morey Barrigan's feet hit the ground, his widened eyes fixed on the rectangular black box.

Slowly the three men approached the

coffin. Barrigan laid a hand on the lid. He paused, took a deep breath . . . then pulled it open.

Jo-Beth Taylor was cleaning tables at the Alpine Café in late afternoon. There were no customers at the moment. The Chinese cook was busy in the kitchen, readying for the supper hour.

Worry gnawed at Jo-Beth's mind, etching deep furrows on her brow. The man she loved was somewhere out there with a cold-blooded killer . . . a man bent on burying Dan Starr in the black coffin. It would be a miracle if the two Barrigan men and Bob Allen reached them in time.

Jo-Beth finished wiping the last table. She released a sigh and brushed back a wisp of blond hair from her eyes. As she moved behind the counter she glanced through the window. People were hurrying excitedly down the street toward the south end of town.

Dashing outside, she saw a crowd gathering around three riders and a wagon. Bob Allen was driving the wagon. Three riderless horses followed on lead ropes. Two of them carried the sacks of stolen gold in their saddlebags. Jo-Beth stood on the boardwalk and breathed, "Thank you, Lord," when she saw that one of the riders was the man she loved.

As the caravan drew abreast of the café Dan smiled at Jo-Beth and halted his mount. Speaking to the others, he said, "See you later, men. I'm stopping here."

Dan let the crowd pass, then swung to the hitching rail and dismounted. As he ducked under the rail Jo-Beth rushed up and embraced him.

"Oh, Dan," she breathed. "I'm so glad you're all right!"

The tall man chuckled. "Me too," he said.

"Where's Curwood?" asked Jo-Beth. "How did you—"

"If you'll get Tinky to whip me up a hot meal, I'll tell you all about it," said Dan. "The other fellows are going home to eat."

While they were waiting they sat at a table and Dan told Jo-Beth the story. Her blue eyes widened as he described how he had been tied to the tree when the cat was coming, with Curwood watching the scene. She hung on every word as he explained how he had leaped into the coffin and watched the angry cougar through the cracks.

Dan had seen the beast run away when Curwood laid a shot near its feet. When he heard rocks cascading down the mountainside, he knew the crazed outlaw would be on level ground shortly. There was a brief moment in his descent when the coffin would be out of his sight.

"I realized if I stayed in the coffin, Curwood had me trapped," Dan explained. "I only had a few seconds, so I climbed out, replaced the lid, and dived into the grave. Curwood shot at the cat when it came at him. I guess the bullet only grazed it. The cat went down. Curwood thought he'd killed it."

Jo-Beth slowly shook her head.

"So, like a wild man, Curwood emptied both of his guns into the coffin, thinking he was filling me full of bullets."

"Oh, Dan!" she gasped, pressing a shaky hand over her mouth.

"Then the cat got up," Dan continued. "It was really mad by that time. It charged Curwood and tore him up something fierce. Even broke his neck. It was still mauling the corpse when Morey and the others rode up and shot it."

Tears flooded the blond woman's eyes. She sprang from her chair and flung her arms around his neck. "Oh, I'm so glad you're all right!" she cried.

Dan stood up and kissed her soundly. Then, holding her tight against him, he chuckled.

"What's so funny?" Jo-Beth asked, her head laid against his chest.

"You should have seen those three guys when I came crawling up out of that grave covered with dirt and splinters!"

Pulling her head back to look at him, Jo-Beth asked, "What about Curwood and his men, Dan? You didn't bring their bodies back."

"Nope," he replied. "We buried them out there where they died."

"Well, what did you do with the black coffin?"

Dan Starr rubbed his stubbly chin. "Well," he replied, devilment in his eyes, "I figured it was Mr. Curwood's coffin, since he paid for it. So we put him in it and buried him in the grave he made me dig."

Then Morey Barrigan entered the café. "Dan," he said, "could you come outside for a moment?"

"Sure, Morey." The tall man grinned. "What's up?"

As Dan and Jo-Beth moved toward the

door, the chairman of Georgetown's governing council said, "Just a little town meeting."

The shadows in the street were growing long where the entire population of Georgetown, Colorado, was gathered. When the man with the badge appeared, a rousing cheer went up, with applause and whistles.

Dan looked down at Jo-Beth, then faced the cheering throng.

Barrigan lifted his hands for silence. When it finally came, he turned to the handsome blond man and said, "Dan Starr, what is that pinned to your shirt?"

"It's a badge, Morey," said Dan, looking down at the metal star on his chest.

"The people of this town have taken a vote, Dan." Barrigan smiled. "We voted unanimously that you wear that badge permanently as our marshal."

Again the crowd cheered and applauded.

"What do you say?" asked Barrigan as the noise subsided.

A warm smile pulled at Dan Starr's lips, and a touch of excess moisture glinted in his eyes. "Thank you, my friends," he said. "I will wear this badge with pride."

Jo-Beth raised her apron, breathed on the badge, and polished it with a flourish.

The citizens of Georgetown gave the marshal an exuberant ovation.

Amid the cheering, Dottie Barrigan moved out of the crowd, accompanied by Merilee John. Dottie said to Jo-Beth, "Honey, you take Dan to your house and fix him a special meal. Merilee and I will cover for you in the café tonight."

Jo-Beth gave Dottie a grateful smile, then turned to her man. "Shall we go, Marshal Dan Starr?" she asked, her eyes beaming.

Georgetown's permanent lawman gave her his arm and moved off the boardwalk. The cheering crowd made a path for them and watched them move up the street in the direction of Jo-Beth's house, looking into each other's eyes.

The sun was dropping over the ragged peaks to the west. A whispering wind funneled off the mountains, skipping along the street, ruffling Jo-Beth Taylor's blonde tresses.

Dottie Barrigan moved close to her husband, taking hold of his hand. "Well, honey," she said, "that's our marshal, the famous Dan Starr."

"Uh-huh," hummed Morey. "And I've got a feeling the little lady on his arm will soon be the famous *Mrs.* Dan Starr!"

The publishers hope that this
Large Print Book has brought
you pleasurable reading.
Each title is designed to make
the text as easy to see as possible.
G.K. Hall Large Print Books
are available from your library and
your local bookstore. Or, you can
receive information by mail on
upcoming and current Large Print Books
and order directly from the publishers.
Just send your name and address to:

G.K. Hall & Co.
70 Lincoln Street
Boston, Mass. 02111

or call, toll-free:

1-800-343-2806

A note on the text
Large print edition designed by
Bernadette Montalvo.
Composed in 16 pt Plantin
on a Xyvision 300/Linotron 202N
by Marilyn Ann Richards
of G.K. Hall & Co.